"She's gotten to yo Nick?"

Dominic Chakiris glanced at Craig Bonner, his friend and vice president of his extensive corporate holdings.

"The only reason I had Kelly MacLeod investigated was to find out why some woman I've never met had the gall to paint a portrait of me and publicly display it."

"I understand there's a waiting list for the privilege of having her do a portrait." Craig grinned. "You should be flattered."

"The portrait is far from flattering. It portrays me as hard and ruthless, a predator ready to pounce on unsuspecting prey."

"Actually, it looks just like you."

Nick shook his head as Craig strolled out of the office. On impulse, he called the unlisted number his investigator had included in Kelly MacLeod's file. He waited through several rings before a sultry voice asked the caller to leave a message.

"This is Dominic Chakiris," he said after the beep. "I believe it's time we met."

Dear Reader,

It's that time of year again…for decking the halls, trimming the tree…and sitting by the crackling fire with a good book. And we at Silhouette have just the one to start you off—Joan Elliott Pickart's *The Marrying MacAllister,* the next offering in her series, THE BABY BET: MACALLISTER'S GIFTS. When a prospective single mother out to adopt one baby finds herself unable to choose between two orphaned sisters, she is distressed, until the perfect solution appears: marry handsome fellow traveler and renowned single guy Matt MacAllister! Your heart will melt along with his resolve.

MONTANA MAVERICKS: THE KINGSLEYS concludes with *Sweet Talk* by Jackie Merritt. When the beloved town veterinarian—and trauma survivor—is captivated by the town's fire chief, she tries to suppress her feelings. But the rugged hero is determined to make her his. Reader favorite Annette Broadrick continues her SECRET SISTERS series with *Too Tough To Tame.* A woman out to avenge the harm done to her family paints a portrait of her nemesis—which only serves to bring the two of them together. In *His Defender,* Stella Bagwell offers another MEN OF THE WEST book, in which a lawyer hired to defend a ranch owner winds up under his roof…and falling for her newest client! In *Make-Believe Mistletoe* by Gina Wilkins, a single female professor who has wished for an eligible bachelor for Christmas hardly thinks the grumpy but handsome man who's reluctantly offered her shelter from a storm is the answer to her prayers—at least not at first. And speaking of Christmas wishes—five-year-old twin boys have made theirs—and it all revolves around a new daddy. The candidate they have in mind? The handsome town sheriff, in *Daddy Patrol* by Sharon DeVita.

As you can see, no matter what romantic read you have in mind this holiday season, we have the book for you. Happy holidays, happy reading—and come back next month, for six new wonderful offerings from Silhouette Special Edition!

Sincerely,

Gail Chasan
Senior Editor

Please address questions and book requests to:
Silhouette Reader Service
U.S.: 3010 Walden Ave., P.O. Box 1325, Buffalo, NY 14269
Canadian: P.O. Box 609, Fort Erie, Ont. L2A 5X3

Too Tough To Tame

ANNETTE BROADRICK

Silhouette®

SPECIAL EDITION™

Published by Silhouette Books

America's Publisher of Contemporary Romance

This book is dedicated to
Donna Hensley who—during computer crashes
(and accompanying tears!)
and helping me to find the parts
that needed to be retyped—stayed calm,
gentle and always on call to explain to
me the mysteries of computers.

The truth is,
I really *couldn't* have done this one without you!

Your grateful cousin…

SILHOUETTE BOOKS

ISBN 0-373-24581-5

TOO TOUGH TO TAME

Copyright © 2003 by Annette Broadrick

This edition published by arrangement with Harlequin Books S.A.

Visit Silhouette at www.eHarlequin.com

Printed in U.S.A.

Books by Annette Broadrick

ANNETTE BROADRICK

believes in romance and the magic of life. Since 1984, Annette has shared her view of life and love with readers. In addition to being nominated by *Romantic Times* as one of the Best New Authors of that year, she has also won the *Romantic Times* Reviewers' Choice Award for Best in its Series; the *Romantic Times* WISH Award; and the *Romantic Times* Lifetime Achievement Awards for Series Romance and Series Romantic Fantasy.

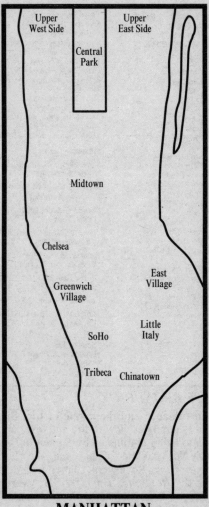

MANHATTAN

Chapter One

October 2003

"She's really gotten to you, hasn't she, Nick?"

Dominic Chakaris glanced over at Craig Bonner, his friend and the vice president of Nick's extensive corporate holdings.

"Hell, no. The only reason I had her investigated was to find out why some woman I've never met had the gall to paint a portrait of me and publicly display it." Nick resumed staring at the view from his office high above the canyons of New York City, his hands in the pockets of his custom-made suit.

"Uh-huh," Craig replied.

Nick turned away from the view and walked to his

desk. His cold gaze met Craig's as both men sat, Craig in front of Nick's massive desk, Nick sprawled in his chair. "What did our investigator find out?" Nick asked.

Craig had known Nick for more than ten years. He wasn't intimidated by the hawklike stare of his esteemed leader. He was probably the only one in Manhattan who could say that and not be lying through his teeth.

Okay, so he should have known Nick would deny that the artist and her portrait of him had been like a thorn in his foot, one that had festered since he'd learned of the painting's existence.

Being a diplomat by nature, Craig said no more. He glanced at the file in his hand and slid it across the desk to Nick, who flipped it open.

"According to our investigator's file," Craig said, "the artist's full name is Kelly Anne MacLeod, age twenty-four. Her parents are dead and she resides alone in the family home on 81st Street. She majored in art history at Vassar. She spent her junior year in Italy and currently brings in a healthy amount of money for the portraits she paints. I understand there's a waiting list for the privilege of having her do a portrait." He lifted one shoulder and grinned. "See, I told you that you should be flattered."

Nick muttered something obscene—causing Craig to laugh—and said, "Is this all you have?" He lifted the few sheets of paper and nodded at the photo attached to the inside cover of the file.

"There wasn't much to discover. She doesn't appear to be a stalker, which you should find immensely reassuring,'' Craig replied, enjoying Nick's discomfort. He was glad not to hear what Nick continued to mutter beneath his breath.

''Nothing here indicates why she chose to place my portrait on public display. Damn it, Craig, I don't care about her orphaned state or how much money she makes. From what I can see,'' he said, closing the file, ''she appears to be like any other debutante, another pampered member of New York's elite.'' A class of people, Nick silently added, that he had little use for. ''And I'm not flattered, as you very well know. Besides, the damned portrait is far from flattering.''

Craig grinned. ''Actually, it looks just like you.''

Nick raised an eyebrow. ''Is that right? The review of her show in the *Times* said that the portrait portrays me as hard and ruthless, a predator ready to pounce on some unsuspecting prey.''

Craig grinned. ''As I said, it looks just like you. Maybe I should take some candid photos of you at one of the board meetings and prove my point.''

Nick stared balefully at his second-in-command and said, ''Since you have little to add to this conversation, I've got work to do.''

''I would imagine that what's really bothering you is the fact that Ms. MacLeod has accurately pegged you and you don't like it. She appears to know you quite well.''

Nick shook his head. ''That's impossible.'' He studied the photograph.

''I doubt that you could forget having met her.''

Craig stood and gave Nick a mock salute before he strolled out of the office.

Nick watched him close the door. He didn't like mysteries…and the reason behind the portrait of him was definitely a mystery. He'd received so many phone calls and comments about the damned thing that he'd gone to the gallery to see what the stir was about…and received the shock of his life.

There was no question that the painting was exceptionally well done, but he couldn't fathom why he'd been chosen as its subject, or why the artist had portrayed him as she had.

There were no photographs of him that resembled the artist's vision. But the painting unnerved him—made him feel as though she'd invaded his privacy.

He focused on the photograph once again. She had pale blond hair and wore it pulled back from her face. Very few women could wear that austere style. Kelly was an exception.

Her intensely blue eyes stared into the camera with humor lurking in their depths. She had the beginnings of a smile curving her lips.

Looking closer, he realized that he had, in fact, seen her before.

He sat back in his chair, put his hands behind his head and recalled the night he'd first noticed her.

He avoided large social occasions as much as possible but in this case he'd felt obligated to go. A business associate had rented one of the city's largest ballrooms to honor his daughter for something. Maybe it was an engagement party.

Nick made it a point whenever he found it necessary to attend such a party to greet the people he knew and listen to any business gossip that reached his ear. Then, once he'd spoken to the host, he left, thankful another painful duty had been fulfilled.

On that night he had paused in the doorway to look over the crowd when he saw her. She was dancing and the light from the chandeliers made her hair look like liquid gold. She'd worn it pulled back to the crown of her head where the soft curls tumbled to her shoulders in studied disarray.

He looked to see if he knew her companion. He didn't. Then he searched for someone that he knew to ask who she was.

By the time he'd struck up a conversation with an acquaintance the song had ended and she'd disappeared.

On his way out of the party a little later she had passed by him within a couple of feet, laughing at something said by one of the women she was with. He'd caught a hint of her light, floral perfume and saw that she was shorter than he'd first thought. Although she looked young, she exuded a self-confidence and grace that intrigued him.

Now he knew who she was. Her name was Kelly MacLeod.

He was intrigued to discover she was the artist who'd painted that damned portrait.

On impulse, Nick placed a call to the unlisted phone number his investigator had included. He waited through several rings before a sultry voice said, ''Hi, this is Kelly. I can't interrupt the temperamental muse to take your call at the moment. Please leave your name, number and any message and I'll get back to you as soon as I escape her clutches.''

"This is Dominic Chakaris," he said after the beep. "I believe it's time that we met in person. Call me at 555-1966."

He hung up and drummed his fingers restlessly on the arm of his executive chair.

Damn, he didn't have time for this. He was already late for a meeting, the outcome of which would determine whether he was going to be spending more than three million dollars on a run-down factory that he wanted.

The intercom rang and he knew his assistant was reminding him of the time. He stood, slid on his suit coat, adjusted his tie and strode out of the room, dismissing Kelly MacLeod from his mind.

"I'm not joking, Hal," Kelly said to her luncheon companion. "I've never met the man, so I'm afraid I can't help you." She took a bite of her salad and casually glanced around the crowded restaurant. Despite the prices, customers flocked to the place—drawn, no doubt, by the excellent chef working his magic in the kitchen.

When she looked back at her companion, she saw that Harold Covington wasn't going to give up. "I've known you your entire life, Kelly," he said as soon as he had her attention, "so don't try to put me off. You could not have produced a portrait that captured the character of the man so brilliantly without knowing him extremely well.''

Kelly met his steady gaze. ''I don't have a rational explanation for you, Hal. I've never been introduced to him, but a person can't pick up a paper without reading something about him in either the business section or the lifestyle section. Plus I've seen him at various social functions during the past few years and had idly thought about what a fascinating subject he would make. That's all it was, an idle thought.

''Then when I discovered that he was behind the takeover of our family business, I couldn't get the man out of my mind. To think that at one time I'd actually admired him! His ruthless disregard for anyone or anything that stands in the way of building his already gigantic empire was responsible for Dad's losing the business and worrying himself into a heart attack. And then mother lost the will to live.

''I decided to work out my anger and grief by painting him. From the feedback I've received, I gather that I've done a good job of portraying the man who destroyed my family!''

Hal sighed and shook his head. ''You were my best hope. All I know is that someone is checking into Covington & Son Industries behind the scenes,'' Hal said. ''It has all the signs of a hostile takeover.''

Kelly paused, her fork halfway to her mouth and said, ''And you think I could walk up to him—even if I knew him—and ask if he's making a run for your company?'' When Hal didn't answer she took a sip of iced tea. ''From everything I've heard about Mr.

Chakaris," Kelly continued after a pause, "only his closest associates know of his plans until after he's swooped down and captured another business."

"I know. It was a long shot to think you knew him well enough to help me."

They had finished their salad before Kelly asked, "Do you really think he's behind whoever's checking into Covington Industries?"

Before Hal could formulate a reply, the waiter arrived with their entrées. Once he left, Hal said, "All I know is that someone appears to be interested in us. You know that the economic downturn has affected many companies. We've all been hard hit. I'm doing what I can to keep my business afloat, but if someone is determined to pursue a takeover they must know how vulnerable the company is right now. I borrowed money to make capital improvements a couple of years ago. If I'd had a crystal ball and known what was coming, I would have postponed them. And now if I were sure Chakaris is planning a takeover, I'd borrow from my wife's family to repay some of those loans—but I don't want to do that unless I absolutely have to. Of course I know that your field of expertise is art, not business. All of this probably makes no sense to you."

Kelly leaned back in her chair and gazed at the man who had been her father's closest friend. "That has to be one of the most patronizing remarks I've ever heard from you, Hal. Next you're going to pat me on the head and suggest I go play in my sandbox while the adults deal with the matter."

Hal flushed. "I'm sorry. I didn't mean my comment to sound that way. As far as that goes, Arnie has a degree in business, sits in on all the board meetings and actually shows up at work two or three days each week. Despite his education and his experience, he shows absolutely no interest in the company. If I had to guess, I would say that you have a better grasp of the business world than he does."

She touched his hand, which lay on the table beside his plate. "I know you're disappointed in Arnold, Hal, but give him time. He's still young."

He looked at her with amused disbelief. "Kelly, he's five years older than you."

She grinned. "Ah, so he is."

"I can't tell you how disappointed I was when the two of you showed no interest in each other. Our families have always been so close. It would have been such a blessing if you had become a member of our family."

Okay, Kelly said to herself, use a little tact here. There was no reason to tell a doting father that his only son and heir was a complete jerk. She couldn't remember ever seeing Arnold Covington completely sober and he went through women faster than the Concorde could cross the Atlantic.

"As you pointed out, my world is considerably different from his," she finally said. She hoped he would assume she was talking about art and business.

"All I'm trying to say is that I have no hard facts to back up my suspicions—just rumors. Chakaris's name has come up more than once. That's usually the only hint an owner gets before he grabs your company out from under you. He's ruthless, you know.''

"Don't forget that I have firsthand knowledge of his tactics, Hal,'' she reminded him.

Once again Hal flushed. "I'm sorry, honey. I wasn't thinking.'' He turned his attention to his food and they lightly chatted through the rest of the meal. Once coffee was served, Hal said, "You seem to be adjusting to being alone these days. I hope that's true and not just an image you're determined to project. I know how close you were to your mother.''

"I know Mom is happy to be with Dad again, Hal. She was never the same after he died. Even though three years had passed, I'll always feel that she died of a broken heart.

"Anyway, with a housekeeper and others looking after the place and caring for me, I'm far from alone.''

"You know what I mean. You must get lonely there.''

"At times, yes, of course. On the upside, I wouldn't have been able to produce enough paintings in time for my showing if I hadn't thrown myself into my work. Staying busy gave me a chance to distance myself from the immediate shock of losing Mother so unexpectedly…until I could better deal with her being gone.''

"So your painting helped you. I'm glad.''

"As a matter of fact, I've set this week aside to go through Mother's belongings. I should have done it sooner, but it was too painful. Anyway, I need to decide what I want to keep and what to give away. Her room is pretty much the way she left it. I know the housekeeper has seen that it's been kept clean, but the actual sorting of her belongings has been left to me. Even though it's been almost a year, I haven't felt I was ready to face that duty before now.''

Kelly glanced at her watch. ''As much as I've enjoyed having lunch with you, Hal, I really need to return home and start on it. The sooner I begin, the sooner the chore will be done.''

Hal stood and pulled out her chair for her. ''And I need to get back as well. I'm sorry I haven't stayed in closer touch with you, my dear. I hope you'll forgive me for being so wrapped up in my own affairs.''

Kelly gave him a quick hug. ''There's nothing to forgive. You've always been only a phone call away. I know if I ever needed you, you'd be there for me.''

Once they were on the sidewalk outside of the restaurant, Hal turned to Kelly and took her hand. ''It was good to see you again, Kelly. We need to do this more often.'' The doorman had signaled for a taxi and when eventually one stopped, Hal put Kelly inside and paid the cabbie as he gave him the address.

She waved at Hal before settling into the seat and thinking about their luncheon conversation. She knew Hal would probably have sought her out anyway, but she was uneasy that he was desperate enough to ask her to spy for him.

If Dominic Chakaris had his eye on Covington & Son, he would be a formidable foe. She could certainly sympathize with Hal.

Once home, Kelly checked her phone messages and found four calls waiting.

A member of one of her mother's charity groups had called to ask Kelly to attend a meeting the next day, no doubt in hopes that Kelly would take over her mother's position.

Another call was from Anita Sheffield, a friend from college she hadn't spoken to in several months. She jotted down her number, sorry she hadn't been there to take Anita's call.

There was a hang up and then she discovered that Dominic Chakaris had left a rather abrupt message. She shivered at the sound of his voice. How strange that he should have called her right after she and Hal had been discussing him.

She played his message over. She wondered how he'd gotten her unlisted number...although a man of his power and connections probably wouldn't have any trouble. No doubt he had a staff of spies to do his bidding.

Not that it mattered. She had more or less expected to hear something from him since she'd placed his portrait in the gallery with her other work.

Hal's question about why she had painted the portrait was one she had repeatedly asked herself during the past several months. Dominic Chakaris had become an obsession with her—her nemesis. His actions had destroyed her family, yet she doubted that he would recognize the family name if she confronted him with it.

Instead of a fruitless confrontation with the man, she

had painted him. Even she had been amazed at how quickly she'd been able to transfer her vision of him to canvas. There had been times when she felt that her hand was guided. She'd worked day and night on the project, barely eating, sleeping for only a few hours at a time before she once again found herself with brush in hand before the canvas.

She remembered the day she'd finished. She'd stood back and looked at the painting as objectively as possible and had known that it was the best work she'd done in her career. She had captured the ruthlessness, the arrogance, that she saw in the man.

However, the expression in his eyes had surprised her. She hadn't thought of him as lonely or vulnerable and yet…there he was, staring back at her, revealing a bleakness that she had never noticed before…at least consciously. She had no idea why she'd painted him that way.

The irony of her present situation was that she had never intended to publicly display the portrait. After all, she had painted it as a catharsis of some kind, to help her get through her grieving process. When Andre, the gallery owner who was presenting an exhibit of her work, had come to her studio to discuss what paintings he wanted to display, she'd given no thought to the painting. Once he'd discovered it buried behind some half-finished canvases, Andre had insisted that she simply must include the portrait in her show. At first she'd been adamant in her refusal, but eventually he'd won the debate. She knew now she should have refused, regardless of Andre's arguments.

She'd convinced herself that Dominic Chakaris would never hear about the portrait. And if he did? He would ignore it…which is what she thought had happened when she'd heard no response from him for several weeks after the opening of her exhibit.

Well, she'd been wrong, hadn't she?

Unwilling to postpone the inevitable, Kelly picked up the phone and dialed the number he'd left.

Chapter Two

The phone was answered on the first ring.

"Chakaris."

Kelly blinked in surprise. The man answered his own phone? She shrugged and said, "This is Kelly MacLeod, returning your call." She couldn't help adding, "Can't you afford to pay for someone to answer your phone?"

There was a pause. She could swear she heard a noise that sounded like a chuckle, which she found odd. He didn't strike her as a man with much of a sense of humor.

"Ah, yes. Ms. MacLeod. Thank you for getting back with me so promptly. The number I left on your machine is my private number. I thought it would save time."

"Save time for what? I take it you wish to discuss the painting?"

"Among other things," he said smoothly. "Would you consider having dinner with me one evening this week?"

He must be kidding. "I don't see why, Mr. Chakaris. If you're interested in buying the painting, I'm sorry. It's not for sale."

"Now, *that's* interesting," he replied. "Although I have no interest in buying it, there are a few things I'd like to discuss with you. If dinner isn't convenient, perhaps we could meet for lunch."

She frowned. Why was he insisting on meeting with her? She was curious—very curious. Well, why not. She'd show him *she* wasn't afraid of him. "When?"

As though there had never been a doubt that she would meet with him, he said smoothly, "Tomorrow, perhaps?"

She did a mental check for possible scheduling conflicts before she replied. "All right."

"Good. I'll send my car for you at twelve-thirty."

"But—" she began, only to hear a dial tone.

She put the phone down and stood there, thinking she probably should have refused.

Don't kid yourself. You've wanted to meet him…it's probably one of the reasons you allowed yourself to be talked into putting the painting on display.

Now there was a bit of nonsense if she'd ever heard one. Kelly checked her watch. She was being ridiculous and had better things to do than analyze her feelings where Dominic Chakaris was concerned.

She would meet him, hear what he had to say and afterward would put him and her painting of him in the past where they belonged.

With a quick shrug, she went upstairs to her mother's bedroom to begin sorting through the last of her mother's possessions.

The next morning Kelly forced herself out of bed, convinced she hadn't slept the night before. She remembered waking up and looking at the clock several times and having trouble going back to sleep.

Part of it was due to her sorting through her mother's things. As much as she had prepared herself, she'd been unnerved by how many memories of her mother had surged back in the course of the afternoon. The slight scent of her mother's favorite perfume lingered in the closet, causing Kelly to feel that her mother was actually there with her.

She'd come across familiar pieces of clothing and had been reminded of the shopping trips she and her mother had shared.

Kelly had found photographs taken of her from the time she was born, all carefully labeled, dated and placed in a leather-bound album.

Her parents looked so happy together, so proud of her, that she could not stop the tears that trickled down her cheeks.

Handling her mother's things reminded Kelly of her loss. Within a four-year period she'd lost both parents. She had watched her mother grieve for her husband, never fully recovering from the loss.

Kelly had developed a hatred for the mammoth corporation that had destroyed her father's health and eventually caused the loss of her mother. Until a few months ago, the greedy corporation and the people behind it had been faceless. Then she had discovered that Dominic Chakaris was the person behind the scenes, playing puppet master with people's lives.

She should have known news of the portrait would eventually reach him.

While she was in the shower, Kelly thought about possible reasons he wanted to meet her. From everything she had learned about the man, she was sure he would take the opportunity to lambaste her for her audacity. He might try to intimidate her into removing the portrait from the show. She decided to launch a preemptive strike.

As soon as she was dressed, she called the gallery. When the manager answered, she said, "Andre, this is Kelly MacLeod."

"Ah, Kelly. I'm glad you called. We've sold two of your paintings since I last spoke with you. We could have sold more if there weren't so many on loan from your clients." He told her which ones and the amount he'd received for them.

"I believe it's time to close my show, don't you?"

"You've done so well, I thought you would want to continue to display your talent in order to gain new clients."

"That's very sweet, Andre, but the truth is, I have a waiting list of women who want their portraits done. Some have managed to get their husbands to agree to a family portrait. If I took no other commissions I'd still be busy for the next couple of years.''

He sighed. ''Then of course I'll do as you wish. I've enjoyed working with you once again. I hope we can do another show for you when you're ready.''

''Of course. I wouldn't have been able to make it this far without your support. The commissions from my first showing after Dad died were a godsend.''

She made arrangements to have the paintings delivered to her the following week and hung up, figuratively brushing her hands for having taken that step.

Later, she heard the doorbell and realized that she'd spent the entire morning in her mother's bedroom without paying attention to the time. She glanced down at her casual clothes and shrugged. She wasn't out to impress the man. If he was offended, too bad.

Nick paced back and forth in front of his desk, checking his watch every few minutes. Ms. MacLeod should be arriving soon and he needed to decide how he would deal with her.

''You're pacing like an expectant father or a nervous bridegroom,'' Craig said, walking into the office. ''Here are the reports you requested, by the way.'' He placed a bundle of bound papers on the desk. ''Maybe they'll help to occupy your mind.''

Nick stared at Craig in disgust. ''Has anyone ever told you that you have an overactive imagination? What makes you think this has anything to do with her? We have several large acquisitions hanging fire at the moment." He nodded toward the papers. "You should know that as well as I."

Craig folded his arms. "Uh-huh. I've known you for years, Nick. You treat the buying and selling done by this company as casually as if you were playing with Monopoly money. The only topic on which I've seen you this nervous is Kelly MacLeod."

Nick walked behind his desk and sat down. "Right," he said rolling his eyes. "Let's see what we have here," he added, pulling the papers toward him.

The chauffeur, who introduced himself as Ben Jackson, was professionally polite as he escorted her to the limousine parked in front of her home. After opening the back door, he helped her inside.

Kelly looked around the spacious interior. The back area was almost as large as some rooms she'd seen. She settled back into the luxurious leather and wondered which restaurant Mr. Chakaris had chosen for this meeting. She wouldn't be surprised if he owned a few.

When the limo stopped some time later Kelly was surprised to see that they were in front of one of the towering office buildings in the business district. She didn't recognize the name on the building. Perhaps it had a restaurant of which she hadn't heard.

The driver came around and opened her door, offering his hand. Once she stepped out of the limo, he escorted her to the doorman and said, "Ms. MacLeod is here to see Mr. Chakaris."

"Of course," the man replied, his uniform giving

him an added measure of dignity. Once inside the cavernous lobby, the doorman handed her off to a man who stood by one of the banks of elevators.

"Ms. MacLeod?" he said with a charming smile. He held out his hand, "I'm Craig Bonner. I'm employed by DCA Industries, Dominic Chakaris's company. It's a pleasure to meet you. I've been impressed with your work for some time." She took his hand and shook it, noticing his firm grip. So Chakaris owned the building. That was the logo she'd seen outside. Why wasn't she surprised?

Craig motioned for her to step into one of the elevators. Kelly had no reason to dislike Mr. Bonner just because he worked for Chakaris and she smiled as she thanked him.

Once the door closed, he pushed one of the buttons before he stepped back to stand beside her.

She looked around. The elevator was spacious and well lit. She wondered if there was a private club in the building. The reclusive Mr. Chakaris would probably prefer a bit of privacy when he dined out, which she would prefer as well. The last thing she needed was to find a comment in tomorrow's gossip columns about having been seen with him.

The doors slid open and her escort ushered her into a large marble foyer. On its walls were three paintings that deserved to be in a museum. In addition, there were several marble busts displayed on Greek columns artistically placed around the area. An ornate flower arrangement in the center of a gleaming table decorated one end of the room. A receptionist sat behind a massive desk at the other end.

Quite an impressive office, she thought. No doubt built with money he'd made cheating rightful owners out of their businesses. Before she could speak she heard a quiet click in the wall opposite the elevator. She turned, and saw tall double doors opening.

"Ms. MacLeod, I'm glad you could meet with me." The man she had spent several weeks painting walked through the doors. He wasn't smiling. She didn't think she'd ever seen that particular phenomenon now that she thought about it.

She would admit, if only to herself, that if this man were anyone other than the man behind the loss of her family, she would have been drawn to him.

He advanced toward her and held out his hand. "Dominic Chakaris."

She reluctantly accepted the hand he offered. As soon as his fingers touched hers she knew she'd made a mistake. The physical contact made her aware of him in a very unsettling way.

She pulled her hand from his. The polite response was to thank him for inviting her but she could not look him in the eye and lie. Instead, she nodded and said, "Mr. Chakaris."

Chakaris glanced around and saw his assistant. "Thanks, Craig," he said as though surprised to find the man still there.

"I'm glad to be of service," Craig replied. He sounded amused, as though at some private joke. Was she missing something here?

Chakaris made a slight—and she was certain mocking—bow toward her and said, "We'll be eating in my private dining room. I thought you might be more comfortable here than in a public restaurant."

As much as she hadn't wanted to be seen with the man, she found the idea of having a private meal with him far from comfortable. She fought not to sound ungracious when she replied. "Whatever's convenient for you."

He motioned toward the open door and she stepped briskly forward, not wishing to have him touch her again.

His corner office overlooked Manhattan and she had to admit the view was spectacular. Two walls were mostly glass. Fine-grained wood covered the other two walls. The same type of wood had been used for his desk. Her artist's eye couldn't help but admire the craftsmanship.

While she took in the size and luxury of the room, Dominic walked over to another door and motioned her to enter.

The dining area was smaller than his office but equally well furnished. A table set for two awaited them. Expensive china, crystal water goblets and sterling silverware gleamed in the light.

"I've ordered our meal ahead of time. I hope you'll approve of my choice." He pulled out one of the chairs for her and once she was seated, sat across from her. "Would you care for wine with lunch?" he asked.

She shook her head. "I prefer iced tea, if it's available."

"Certainly." He must have pushed some hidden button because a tall, slender man opened a nearby door.

"Yes, sir?"

"You may serve us now, Dimitrios. We'll have iced tea."

The man nodded and left the room, leaving them alone once again. Kelly had been in many social situations in her life, but she couldn't remember one where she'd felt so awkward.

Dominic picked up his water glass and held it out to her. "I'd like to make a toast. May this be the beginning of a beautiful friendship."

Kelly had reached for her glass—not so much to join him in his toast, but because her mouth was so dry—when he spoke. Thank goodness she hadn't taken a sip. Otherwise, his audacity would have caused her to spray water over everything.

She lifted an eyebrow and said, "A friendship, Mr. Chakaris? I hardly think so. I'm afraid I don't know your reason for insisting on having this meeting. I've instructed the gallery to remove your portrait, which was the only thing I could think of to explain it."

He paused with the glass halfway to his mouth. "I'm hoping you can satisfy my curiosity as to why I became a subject for your artistic endeavors." He sipped from the glass, his gaze steady.

"Consider it an aberration. I'd lost my mother and was dealing with a lot of emotional stuff. Call it therapy if you will."

Chakaris looked startled by her explanation. Before

he could comment, Dimitrios entered carrying a tray of food. After setting their plates and tea in front of each of them, he asked, ''Will there be anything else, sir?''

Chakaris scanned the table quickly before saying, ''I believe we have everything. Thank you.''

Except an appetite, Kelly thought ruefully. She'd had some misguided notion that she would be able to answer his questions in a calm, unemotional manner. Instead, her stomach felt tied in knots and she could feel one of her tension headaches coming on.

After a moment she picked up her fork and took careful bites of her food, which tasted like ambrosia, melting in her mouth. Before she knew it, she had finished her lunch.

She'd been relieved that he'd chosen not to continue their discussion while they ate. Once they were drinking their coffee, Chakaris said, ''Shall we go into my office? I'm intrigued to learn why you chose me to— er—help you deal with your grief.'' He rose and politely pulled her chair out.

Kelly walked into the office and stood in the middle of the room, cupping her elbows in her hands. Instead of walking to his desk, Dominic strode to the other side of the room where there was a grouping of leather chairs and a sofa.

He motioned to one of the chairs. ''Please have a seat, Ms. MacLeod. I'd like to know why you painted that damned portrait.''

Kelly dropped her arms and with a slight lift of her

chin walked over to the chair and sat down. Only then did he take the other chair.

"What if I told you my reasons are private. Would you respect that?" she asked quietly.

He didn't answer right away. Instead, he looked at her as though working out a puzzle. Finally, he replied softly. "You apparently felt no similar need to protect *my* privacy."

He had a good point, she silently admitted. She wondered what to tell him. Stalling for time, Kelly said, "You should be flattered. After all, some women find you very attractive."

He waved the remark away as though swatting a fly. "Don't patronize me, Ms. MacLeod."

Kelly was reminded of her response to Hal. Perhaps there was some truth in her adversary's challenge.

Before she could decide how to respond, he said, "I'd appreciate hearing the truth."

The truth. The truth had many facets. She wondered why she was stalling. This man's ruthless determination to get whatever he wanted was legendary and he wanted the truth. She had no need to protect his feelings…if he had any.

Kelly squared her shoulders and looked him in the eye. "All right. Here's the truth for you, Mr. Chakaris. I painted your picture in an effort to exorcise my anger at your methods of making money. My father's death four years ago was the direct result of your ruthless business practices. My mother was never the same once he was gone. Thanks to you, I've lost both of them. So the portrait was an effort to deal with some of my anger and hatred of you."

Chapter Three

Nick knew he had enemies. He'd had to fight hard to get where he was and he'd stepped on a few toes along the way, but he had never been accused of single-handedly destroying someone's family.

There was nothing about Kelly MacLeod's demeanor to make him think she was mentally unhinged and she obviously believed what she was saying.

The last time he'd seen her was a few weeks ago when he glanced around from a conversation to see her watching him. She'd immediately returned her attention to her friends.

If he'd known she was the artist of the infamous painting, he would have made an effort to speak to her.

Nick was a little disappointed that her interest in him was negatively based because she intrigued him.

He'd always dated tall brunettes with dark eyes. He would never have guessed that he would be attracted to a petite woman with vivid blue eyes and light blond hair. Yet he definitely was attracted to her and had been since the first moment he saw her years ago.

Kelly made no effort to speak. She appeared calm sitting on the edge of her chair so primly, her ankles crossed and hands folded, appearing as though their discussion was about the latest fund-raising event.

Nick leaned back in his chair. When he spoke, his tone was dry. "I have to say your unflattering portrayal of me was a unique way of expressing your rather violent emotions toward me."

"Of course you would consider all of this a joke."

"Not at all. What business did your father own?"

"The Angus MacLeod Company, started by my great-great-grandfather in the late 1800s. He converted the factory for military use during wartime. Afterward, he went back to domestic manufacturing. The factory had been in our family for years…until you decided to add it to your collection."

At least he had something tangible to follow up on. He picked up the phone on the table by his elbow. When his assistant answered, he said, "Evelyn, please have the files on The Angus MacLeod Company sent in as soon as possible." He hung up and looked at Kelly. "I'll be better prepared to discuss this matter with you once I've seen the files. May I get you something to drink while we're waiting?"

Kelly worried her bottom lip with her teeth. There was really no reason for her to stay. It was obvious he had no recollection of what he had done. Why wasn't she surprised? she thought bitterly. Her throat was dry, she admitted to herself. With a brief nod, she replied, ''Water, please.''

He stepped to a nearby wall and pushed a hidden button, causing the wall to move and reveal a well-stocked bar. Everything anyone could possibly want was at his fingertips.

He returned with a crystal glass filled with ice and water.

''Thank you,'' she said, taking a sip.

He sat across from her once again and said, ''Tell me about your father, if you will.''

''I know none of this means anything to you, but my father was an unusually gifted man. He had a keen appreciation of art and history and was an expert on sixteenth-century English writers. I could not have asked for a more nurturing, loving father.''

Dominic knew the kind of man she described. Many owners of family companies that were barely surviving were like her father. He wondered how to point out to Kelly that being an erudite man in no way qualified her father to run a successful business.

''He sounds like a fine gentleman, Kelly, but nothing you've said speaks to his business acumen.''

''He worked diligently at the factory his entire life. He was conscientious and did everything he could to make the business succeed.''

''Your father inherited a thriving business, is that correct?''

She stiffened. ''Yes.''

"In general, I've found that many family-owned companies are run by a family member who has no idea how to run a business. You mentioned that your father's interests lay elsewhere." He paused, carefully choosing his words. "Without educating himself in the field of business, a person would have little concept of how to keep a company going. Perhaps your father was a hands-on owner. I won't know until I've seen the file, but many owners in similar situations allow others to do the day-to-day supervision. A manager might suggest spending capital to modernize the business, but new technology is expensive. Perhaps your father allowed the business to continue without investing more money in it. Of course this is all speculation on my part."

"My father was diligent about keeping informed. He wouldn't have let the business run down. Yes, Mr. Chakaris, it is obvious that you never knew my father." Kelly stood and walked to the wide expanse of glass that gave a bird's-eye view of Manhattan, her arms gripped tightly against her stomach. Without turning, she said, "My father was a man of integrity. In addition, he was not a lavish spender."

Dominic walked toward her, his hands in his pockets. "You're welcome to believe that, of course, but it has been my experience that a home such as yours takes a great deal of money to own and maintain, not to mention the cost of your private schooling and a year abroad studying art."

She spun around, startled to find him so close. "That's another thing. You had no right to have me investigated. There is no way you could know about my education without prying into my life. I know *exactly* what my education cost, Mr. Chakaris, as well as the cost of maintaining my home. Once Dad was gone, Mom and I discovered how precarious our financial situation was. Knowing him, Dad wouldn't have wanted us to worry about any of this, which is why he'd never discussed the business with either of us. Don't you know that if I had known, I would never have continued my studies? I've had to live with that knowledge since he died. In order to care for us, he borrowed money from the bank. He took no money from the factory. He would never have put the factory into jeopardy."

Nick clenched his jaw before he said something he might later regret. Her temper was finally showing through her icy demeanor but he refused to be baited by a grieving woman who didn't know what she was talking about. He glanced at his watch, wondering where the hell those files were.

He was irritated with himself for having gotten into a discussion about a particular business of his before bringing himself up to date on it.

Finally, he spoke in a quiet voice. "I'm sure your father was a good man. Since I'm not interested in acquiring a business until and unless it's obvious that it's failing, my guess is that, despite his sterling qualities, he wasn't able to keep his company going."

There was a tap on the door and Nick turned away with relief. "Come in," he said.

He was surprised to see Craig until he spotted the thick file in his hand. He lifted a questioning brow.

"Sorry it took so long to pull the file. The name's been changed and we've owned it for several years."

Nick didn't look at Kelly. "That's fine, Craig. Sorry to pull you away from your work."

"No problem." Craig left the room and Nick sat behind his desk. For reasons he didn't quite want to admit, he half hoped to find that he had been wrong about this particular transaction. Not that it was his aim in life to destroy anyone. He owed no one an apology for rescuing failing businesses. He'd built his fortune that way and he was good at it.

He gave a mental shake and opened the file. Kelly continued to stand. With a silent sigh, Nick motioned her to one of the chairs in front of him. "Please have a seat. I need to scan this. It won't take long, I promise."

With obvious reluctance Kelly sat, watching him closely.

He read the summary of the shape the business was in when he took it over as well as the amount of money he'd paid for it.

Nick closed the file and looked at Kelly. She was watching him as though he were a wild animal about to pounce.

He considered himself a damned good negotiator. However, he'd never been in a situation like this one before. It was no surprise that Kelly MacLeod's emotions were running high at the moment. He didn't want to upset her further, but he also didn't want to have her leave his office without knowing the facts.

"When we first heard about the MacLeod property, the place was no more than a month away from shutting its doors."

She opened her mouth as though to object, so he handed her the Angus MacLeod company's balance sheet for the last year before his firm took it over.

"It isn't my intention to add to your grief by going into the details of this transaction. I accept that your father was devastated by the loss of his company. However, he would have lost it whether or not I bought it." He glanced down at the file. "I don't normally allow anyone other than my employees to look at files, but I'm going to make an exception this time." He moved the file closer to her and waited while she looked over the documents inside.

He was bending over backward in order to show Ms. MacLeod that he was not responsible for her father's losing his business.

There were documents in the file that reported the financial status of the company five years ago, along with copies of several promissory notes signed by her father at various times, using the business as collateral.

An itemized profit-and-loss statement for each of the five years before the company was taken over showed a steady and consistent loss of revenue.

As soon as she looked up from the file he said, "When I took it over, the business was worth very little. As you see, your father received more than a fair price for what was left of his business. What he chose to do with the money was his concern.

"I understand the pain of losing your parents, Ms. MacLeod, and you may have found some relief in finding someone you could blame. However, I will not apologize for my business practices. I had no control over your father's choices, nor over his willingness to go deeper into debt when he knew he had a snowball's chance in hell of being able to repay those loans. He made his choices and he had to live with them."

Kelly rubbed her temple as though her head ached. "When he died," she finally said as she continued to study the documents, "Mom and I thought we had a certain amount of financial security until I found out what had been going on." She pointed to the documents. "He must have paid off those notes with money he received when you took over. We paid other debts with his life insurance policy."

He said nothing more. The papers had upset her, that was obvious, but what was he supposed to do? Let her irrational assumptions continue without an attempt to point out the flaws in her thinking?

Finally, she looked at him and said, "In my own defense, I didn't deliberately make the painting of you unflattering. I painted what I saw."

He quirked an eyebrow. "What you saw from attending the same benefits and other social functions I attended? Without once attempting to speak to me or find out anything about me? You may have painted what you saw but only through the emotional filters of who you decided I am."

''Perhaps you're right. In any case, the portrait is no longer on display.'' Kelly stood and moved toward the door.

Nick followed her. He hoped to lighten the mood somewhat and said, ''I've been assured by those who know me that your portrait perfectly captured my personality. I have hopes that my ego will eventually recover from that rather lowering assessment.''

She turned and looked at him in surprise at his attempt at humor. He didn't want her thinking of him as an ogre. He was merely a businessman who had done well by making decisions based on facts and figures, not emotions.

He reached the door first and swung it open for her. ''I'm sorry that our first meeting was an adversarial one. I'd like to start over, if possible. Would you be willing to have dinner with me sometime when my business practices won't be the topic of conversation?''

She looked him over dismissively before she replied, ''I would enjoy having dinner with you Mr. Chakaris…as soon as hell freezes over.''

Chapter Four

The next morning Kelly paused and stepped back from the canvas she was currently finishing. She was having trouble concentrating, which wasn't surprising. She'd been rattled since she'd left Dominic Chakaris's office.

The painting wasn't going well. She decided to leave it alone before she did something irreversible to it. Kelly cleaned her brushes and afterward absently settled into one of the window seats.

The more she had listened to Dominic Chakaris calmly explain that his business tactics were reasonable and logical, the more upset she had become. She'd been unable to sleep much of the night for thinking about the cold-blooded way the man did business.

No wonder Hal Covington was concerned. Like her father, Hal had inherited his business. He'd done well, though, and she couldn't understand why he was worrying about the possibility of his company being taken over. If Chakaris was being truthful, he didn't go after successful businesses.

Despite her dislike of him, she believed him, mostly because he didn't care enough about any of this to bother to lie.

Somebody needed to stand up to him, to show him that life was more than assets and liabilities. People were more important, something he seemed to ignore.

When she'd finally crawled out of bed this morning, she'd formed a plan of sorts. Supposing she did accept his invitation.

Could she see him again without revealing her aversion to him? What if she could help her father's old friend by discovering whether Chakaris was considering Hal's company as a potential acquisition?

She would have to think about that. Finding her way into the enemy's camp could backfire. She had to decide whether the risks were worth it.

Kelly decided that if she couldn't concentrate on her work, she would finish sorting through her mother's belongings.

Several hours later she heard the doorbell ring. She glanced at her watch. It was after one o'clock. As far as she could recall, no one had planned to stop by today. Her curiosity drew her to the hallway overlooking the foyer and she watched as Bridget answered the door.

Kelly couldn't see who was there but when Bridget stepped back she was holding a large floral arrangement. She closed the door and started for the stairs. Kelly met her halfway and took the flowers.

"Thank you, Bridget."

"It's been some time since you received flowers, hasn't it?"

Kelly smiled. "True. And I haven't the foggiest idea who could have sent them now." As she turned to go back upstairs, she suddenly knew who had sent the elaborate arrangement. She carried it to her room and placed it on a table between two windows.

The large bouquet was a colorful mixture of fragrant flowers and she had to admit they brightened the room. She reached for the card and drew it out of the envelope. The note read,

The latest forecast predicts an arctic front moving through hell. I thought the ensuing freeze might give you a reason to have dinner with me Saturday.

Nick

Nick. She hadn't realized he went by a nickname. It seemed out of character, somehow. She studied the card and realized that he must have personally chosen the bouquet to have written the message. His writing was bold, slashing across the card.

Her phone rang. Absently she picked it up.

"Hello?"

"You received my flowers," a deep voice said in her ear.

"Are you lurking outside my home?"

"Not at all. I told the florist to have them delivered promptly. I felt certain they would have arrived by now."

If he but knew it, he had given Kelly the opportunity she needed if she decided to follow through with her plan to help Hal. Did she have the nerve? Did she really want to be around Chakaris again?

Stalling for time, she replied, "I suppose you own the florist shop."

There was a brief silence before he said, "As a matter of fact, I do. The shop is here in the building."

"Is there anything in this city you *don't* own, Mr. Chakaris?"

"Please call me Nick. And yes, there are a great many things in this city over which I have no control."

"That's reassuring," she said dryly. "That should keep your ego somewhat in check."

"My ego is already suffering from the shellacking you gave it yesterday. I was hoping for the opportunity to convince you I'm not really the monster you seem to think I am."

Had he always sounded so sexy? She'd been too agitated yesterday to notice...or at least had done her best not to consider his physical attributes.

She swallowed. "Saturday?" she repeated faintly. Three days from tonight? Could she do it? She studied the calendar near her phone.

"I have business meetings back to back until then.

I'll be distracted, I'm sure, thinking about you, but I'll force myself to sit through them.''

She rolled her eyes at the obvious line. "I'm afraid I can't on Saturday. I already have plans.''

He didn't respond right away and she wondered if he'd hung up when he said, ''I would really like to see you again. Is it possible that we could start over from here and see what develops?''

''I'm available Sunday evening,'' she said with reluctance.

''Good. I'll be there at seven.''

She hung up thoughtfully. If this were anyone but Dominic Chakaris, she might get the idea that he was personally interested in her, but she knew that Chakaris, the corporate raider, would see her simply as a challenge. Even if he were interested in her, he would soon move on to his next conquest. He had a reputation for refusing to become seriously involved with anyone.

In any case, she was committed to spending only one evening with him—to having dinner, nothing more. If she intended to help Hal—and wasn't that the reason she'd given herself for agreeing to see Dominic again?—she would need to be around him more.

That being the case, she'd taken the first step.

Saturday evening, William Comstock III arrived on time to take her to the benefit dance for one of her mother's charities.

''You're ready?'' Will asked, placing his hand over his heart in surprise.

"Very funny," she replied. "As though you've ever had to wait for me."

He hit his forehead with the palm of his hand. "Oooh, *that's* right. I must have you confused with one of my other women." He stepped back and looked at her. "Great outfit. I'm not going to ask how you manage to keep the top up."

She shook her head and grinned. Will had dated Anita, her college roommate, during which time he and Kelly had become best buds. Their friendship had outlasted the romantic one. Since his family insisted he attend so many of these functions, Kelly and Will had made a pact to go together and "guard each other's back," as Will so quaintly put it.

Kelly was glad for his undemanding companionship tonight. Had her date been anyone else she would probably have cancelled. Instead she'd bought a new dress—black sheer with a silk lining. When she first saw it she had wondered, like Will, if she'd be able to lift her arms to dance without losing the bodice. She was amazed at the masterful engineering that had gone into the dress to prevent such a thing from happening.

Will opened the door and escorted her to his late-model roadster. "Hope you don't mind if we don't stay long. I'm promised to someone else tonight." Kelly laughed, as he knew she would. "How about you?" he asked once he was behind the wheel. "Has some lucky guy swept you off your feet and promised you the world?"

"Not yet. I can always hope," she replied, chuckling. "Of course you know that's not true. I have too much to do to encourage a relationship right now."

"Uh-huh. That's what you've been telling me since you graduated. If you don't accept some invitations soon I'm going to drag every single male I know over here for your inspection and review and insist you go out with each one at least once."

"You wouldn't!" Kelly said, mortified. "What a horrible thought. Besides, you needn't worry about me. I actually have a dinner date tomorrow night."

Will threaded his way through heavy traffic. He glanced at her in surprise. "No kidding! Somebody I know?"

"I doubt it."

"So who is he? C'mon, Kelly. I keep you up to date on my love life. Don't be shy."

"I'm not being shy. And this isn't about a love life. It's just a dinner date, for Pete's sake."

"Ah, you're going out with Pete, are you?" He waited a couple of seconds and asked, "Pete who?"

She hit his arm. "You idiot. I don't know why I put up with you...I really don't."

"I do," he said, suddenly sounding serious. "You feel safe with me. I've known that for years. If I ever made a pass at you, you'd take off so fast you'd leave skid marks."

"I'm not going to discuss this anymore," she said with dignity. "Besides, we're here," she added with relief as he swung into the valet parking area in front of the hotel.

"Fine with me. We can sit here in the car all evening as far as I care. Who is he?"

"Oh, all right," she said with irritation. "It's Dominic Chakaris." She smiled as one of the parking attendants opened her door. She waited for Will near the entrance and he soon joined her. He took her elbow and escorted her into the hotel.

"Oh, all right. If you're going to make up somebody, I give up. All I'll say is you must be ashamed of him if you have to keep him a secret."

She grinned, suddenly in a better humor. "This time, I'm telling you the truth. It *is* Dominic Chakaris."

They paused as the other invitees moved ahead of them into the ballroom. "Oh, yeah. I believe you. The man you hate, the man you painted with so much ferocity that I felt sorry for the poor canvas at times? This is the guy you're going to see?"

She chuckled, her eyes on his face as they entered the ballroom. "What can I say," she replied, fluttering her eyelashes at him, "the poor man was swept away by me. I wouldn't be surprised if by the end of tomorrow night he isn't pleading with me to have his children!"

Nick saw her as soon as she walked through the door, his head turning like a magnet to the north. The strong surge of lust at the sight of her caught him off guard. Not that he should be surprised. Wearing that dress, she was going to cause every man in the place to suffer whiplash. The dress, what little there was to it, clung to her as though it were wet, emphasizing her bare shoulders, her gentle curves and very attractive legs. She looked small as she stood beside Adonis... the top of her head barely came to her partner's shoulder. And who the hell was he? In addition to his good looks, he had the build of an athlete, with broad shoulders and slim hips. His blond hair fell boyishly across his forehead and he looked at home in a tuxedo.

Nick fought to get control of his unruly body. He'd never had such an embarrassingly public reaction to a woman in his life and it would have to be triggered by Kelly MacLeod, of all people.

He'd asked her out again despite her unflinching refusal because he hoped to overcome her hostility toward him by allowing her to get to know him better...or at least become neutral toward him. Yes, he'd found her to be attractive, and yes, he'd entertained the idea of taking her to bed eventually, but his strong reaction just now rattled him.

He had a cavemanlike urge to rush to her, throw her over his shoulder, beat his chest so that everyone in the room knew that she belonged to him, and take her home with him...where he would keep her in his bed for as long as his stamina held.

Nick closed his eyes and rubbed his forehead; the beginning of a headache was making itself known. As soon as he opened them, he immediately searched until he found her again. He kept his eyes trained on the couple as they paused to greet first one group, then another.

They looked so comfortable together. The casual intimacy between them jarred him.

Damn.

Well, what did you think, Chakaris? That you're the first man to notice her? Males had probably been following her around since preschool.

"I say, Chakaris, have you heard a word I've said?" One of the stuffed shirts he'd been listening to grumbled. Nick had a hell of a time being polite in these situations. Everyone was so taken with his own self-importance, it was a wonder there was enough space in the ballroom for all the egos on display.

"If you'll excuse me," Nick murmured to the group of men, "I just saw someone I need to speak with." Without waiting for a reply, Nick moved purposefully through the crowd to reach Kelly.

"Now this is getting interesting," Will said to Kelly as they turned toward the buffet table.

"What is?"

He slipped his arm around her waist and leaned down, nuzzling her ear and saying, "The man whose babies you're going to have is headed straight for us…and the look on his face suggests pistols at dawn."

Kelly tried to pull away from him, but Will's grip was too firm. She turned her head just as Nick appeared beside her.

"Good evening, Kelly," Nick said in a polite voice. "I'd like to meet your escort, if I may."

Kelly saw a nerve twitching in his jaw. Good grief. What was that about? "Will," she said coolly, "I'd

like you to meet Dominic Chakaris.'' She looked at
Nick. ''This is William Comstock III.''

More unwelcome news, Nick thought wryly. He
happened to know that name. Even if every member
of the family was a spendthrift, there was enough
money in the Comstock coffers to last several life-
times.

He nodded without offering his hand and returned
his gaze to Kelly. ''I find the gown you're almost
wearing quite eye-catching.''

He saw Kelly stiffen but before she could reply, her
escort said, ''That's what I've been telling her. I offered her some Scotch tape to help with the strapless
top, but she wouldn't hear of it.''

Kelly tried not to laugh but failed. Will was incorrigible. ''Thank you,'' she said to Nick. ''The dress is
sturdier than it looks,'' she added smoothly.

Nick nodded. ''I won't keep you from the buffet.''
He nodded to Will once again, then to her, and got
the hell away from her before he made a complete ass
of himself.

What had he been thinking, making such a personal
remark to her? Despite her escort being taller than
Nick by a good three inches, Nick had been ready to
take a swing at Comstock for having his arm around
her waist.

Had he lost his frigging mind?

Nick looked around the room. Most of the faces
were familiar to him because the same people invari-
ably attended these things. What the hell. He was one
of them now, wasn't he? Why should he sneer when

he'd deliberately and systematically carved a niche for himself in their world?

It was time for another drink.

After dinner an orchestra began to play and several couples moved onto the dance floor and started dancing to the rhythm of the music.

Will and Kelly shared a table with several acquaintances who were used to seeing them together. Several lively discussions took place throughout dinner and the group was still talking when the music started.

Kelly leaned toward Will and murmured, "Are you ready to go?"

"Are you kidding?" he replied with a grin. "I wouldn't miss any of this for the world."

"Miss any of what?"

"The way Chakaris keeps his eye on you no matter where you are. With every move we've made, he's made a corresponding move in order to keep you in his line of sight."

Kelly refused to look around but she could feel her cheeks burning. "I'm glad you're having so much fun imagining things. The man barely knows me."

"That may be true, but not from lack of trying, I bet. So what did you do? Break down and finally agree to go out with him?"

A sudden memory of the bouquet of flowers he'd sent flashed into her mind and she continued to blush.

"Oh, ho," Will hooted softly. "That's what this is about. You're doing everything just right, you know.

Make him chase you. Make him work for your attention."

"How much have you had to drink tonight?" she demanded in a low voice, so that the others couldn't hear. "You've taken one tiny fact and built a whole fantasy world from it!"

Will glanced over her shoulder and whispered, "We'll see, won't we?" In a normal tone, he said, "Enjoying the party, Chakaris?"

Kelly's head whipped around. Nick stood a couple of feet away and she had the horrifying thought that he might have heard their discussion. She hoped they had been speaking quietly enough that no one had caught Will's ridiculous comments.

"It's all right," Nick responded, his eyes on Kelly. "Would you care to dance?"

"Oh, I, uh, that is—"

"She'd be pleased to dance with you, wouldn't you, Kelly, love?" Will said with a perfectly straight face. It was all she could do not to punch him in the shoulder.

As gracefully as possible, Kelly rose and walked toward the dance floor. When she turned, Nick was immediately behind her. He took her in his arms and they moved into a gliding step, as though they had danced together for years.

Nobody had ever mentioned in her hearing that this man could dance like a professional. He held her at a proper distance, his hand casually resting at the small of her back. With a relaxed and casual skill, Nick guided her around the ballroom. She found him easy to follow and began to relax in his arms.

He was the perfect height for her to dance with. She was wearing three-inch heels, and her eyes were level with his chin. Nick said nothing as the music worked its magic through her. Kelly settled into the rhythm of the song and flowed with him.

At some point the music segued into a slow, bluesy kind of number. It seemed natural for him to pull her closer and wrap his arms around her. Kelly slid her arms around his neck and placed her head on his shoulder.

As her body was pressed against him, Kelly realized he was fully aroused. He wanted her—that was obvious. Or maybe his reaction was strictly physical. Perhaps this happened with every woman with whom he danced. She drew back slightly so that she was not in such intimate contact.

Moving in Nick's arms in time to the music seemed to be the most natural thing in the world. Kelly felt drugged...seduced by the music and the man. She tried to work up her usual antagonism against him but for now it had disappeared.

When the music ended, Kelly needed a moment to come back to the here-and-now. Nick seemed to have the same problem as he reluctantly released her.

Kelly made the mistake of looking at him and saw the heated expression in his eyes. She could feel herself flush and knew her fair skin betrayed her agitation.

He lifted her hand and brushed his lips across her

knuckles. "Thank you for dancing with me," he said quietly.

She couldn't seem to look away from him. In an uneven tone she replied, "You're a wonderful dancer." Kelly waited for a look of satisfaction to appear on his face at her words. Instead, he gave her hand a soft squeeze and led her back to her table.

Will was also returning to the table and saw them. "I hate to call this short, but I need—"

"Of course," she rushed in to say. "It's getting late and I should get home as well."

With a brief nod to Nick, Will encircled her shoulders and crossed the room, heading for the door.

Nick watched them go, feeling as though something had been ripped out of his heart when she disappeared from his view. Now there was a joke. There were many people who would swear he had no heart.

He'd always agreed with them.

Until now.

Chapter Five

William said nothing until they were in his car and on the way to her home. Kelly appreciated his silence. Her head was swimming with so many conflicting thoughts she could find nothing coherent to say.

What had happened back there? Had she actually forgotten who Chakaris was and the damage he had done to her...as well as others?

As if her thoughts weren't confusing enough, her emotions clamored for attention. She relived how she'd felt with his arms around her and the hint of aftershave mixed with the distinctive—and indescribable—scent of a clean, healthy male. How could she have become so caught up in her senses?

When they reached her home, Will escorted her to the door and waited while she unlocked it. When she turned to say goodbye, Will said, "All kidding aside, Kelly. I want you to be careful where Chakaris is concerned. I thought you two were going to burn the place down with the heat you were generating on the dance floor. It's obvious that Chakaris has you in his sights." He lifted her chin with his finger. "Don't let his charm and sex appeal lull you into forgetting that the man's dangerous. We both know that. I know none of this is my business, but I can't help worrying about you. We've been friends for a long while and I'd hate like hell to see you get hurt.

"I know that you're an adult and capable of making rational, mature decisions. You need to keep in mind that he's as ruthless as your portrait reveals him to be."

She leaned her head against his chest. "Thanks for caring, Will. I value our friendship and your wise counsel. You needn't worry, though. I'm fully aware of who and what Dominic Chakaris is. I can never forget that. I promise I'll be all right." She pulled away from him and forced herself to smile. "Now go see your latest flame before she gets tired of waiting for you."

Once inside, Kelly closed the door behind her and leaned against it, wondering if she could force her trembling knees to carry her up the staircase. She had to get a grip on her emotions. She was being ridiculous. She'd been around other attractive men before, men who had made their desire for her known in various ways. To have such a strong reaction to this particular male made no sense at all.

By the time she'd crawled into bed, Kelly had convinced herself that she'd suffered some kind of momentary aberration. A good night's sleep would restore her once again to sanity.

The problem, she discovered the next morning, was that she hadn't been able to rest well. She had dozed and dreamed and tossed and turned until dawn, when she finally gave up and went downstairs to the kitchen for much-needed coffee.

The first thing she would do after stoking up on her daily ration of caffeine would be to contact Chakaris and cancel their dinner tonight. It was only after her third cup of coffee had kicked in that she remembered the only number she had was his private office number. Despite his reputation as a workaholic she really didn't think he would be there. She had nothing to lose by trying, though.

The phone rang once and voice mail kicked in with Nick saying curtly, "Leave a message."

She actually considered doing just that, until she realized she wouldn't know whether or not he got it. As the morning progressed she finally accepted that she would dine with him tonight. What did she think could happen in a crowded restaurant, after all? They would eat and she would return home and that would be the end of her association with him. Despite what she had told Will, she knew that she was susceptible to Nick's charm. Although she wanted to help Hal, she didn't have a clue how to find out business information for him.

Functioning on too little sleep or not, she could do

this. She'd always confronted everything in life head-on. There was no reason for her to change now.

Kelly was in the study that evening when the limousine arrived. As soon as she heard the doorbell Kelly called to Bridget, "I'll get it." When she opened the door, Kelly was brought up short. Nick Chakaris stood there.

"I thought you were the driver."

He lifted one eyebrow without changing expression. "No. I'm your escort."

All right. So that was a rather inane thing to say, she thought. She reminded herself to sharpen up, to consider this evening as a business meeting.

"Yes, I can see that." Kelly stepped through the doorway, turned and locked the door behind her, then allowed Nick to guide her down the steps and into the waiting car.

Once settled inside, he said, "I trust you've recovered from the benefit last night."

"I'm fine, thank you."

"I'm curious to know how long you and Comstock have been seeing each other."

Seeing each other? So he thought she was involved with Will, did he? That might work to her advantage. Let's face it, she thought, she needed all the advantages she could get.

"We met in college," Kelly replied. "Where are we going tonight?"

"I'm keeping it a surprise. I guarantee the food will be the best there is. The chef is exceptional." He paused, as though searching for words. Finally, said, "I appreciate your willingness to call a truce."

She glanced at him before returning her gaze to the window. "Is that what this is?"

"I sincerely hope so. I did everything I could to see that hell froze over this evening. I'm grateful you gave me the benefit of the doubt."

"You must be pleased with my capitulation."

"With your willingness to consider a truce," he gently corrected. "I enjoyed dancing with you last night. I had difficulty seeing you leave with someone else. The only consolation I had was to know that I would see you tonight...without Comstock."

No red-blooded woman could hear that from an attractive man without her heart beating a little faster. She found it prudent not to respond.

"By the way," he said when she remained silent, "I'm curious to know what you did with the portrait since it was removed from the gallery."

She turned and looked at him, wanting to appear as cool and composed as he was. "Why do you care?" she asked coolly.

"Oh, I just wanted to know if you were using it now for dart practice."

"Something like that."

He shifted in his seat so that he could see her better. "Tell me something about yourself," he invited.

She gave him a sideways glance. "I'm sure you have all the information you need about me in your dossier."

"Ouch," he replied. "I was hoping you would forgive me for that."

"As well as for the fact my parents are gone?"

That must have gotten to him, she thought. She saw a muscle jump in his jaw.

"I understand your grief," he finally replied. "If you choose to ignore the facts and hang on to your prejudicial view of me, I can't stop you. However, I was hoping we could release the past and start over with each other."

She glanced at him, then quickly away.

"Are you a native of New York?" he asked.

She could continue to bait him—which could prove to be somewhat dangerous. Pulling a tiger's tail wasn't the safest thing to do, after all. Or she could answer his question. After weighing her options, Kelly said,

"I was born in Manhattan. What about you?"

"I was born in the Bronx."

She was still digesting that piece of news when the limousine stopped. She looked outside and discovered they were in front of Nick's office building. She frowned. Now what?

Nick helped her from the car and escorted her inside the building. With a brief nod to the security guard Nick guided her into one of the elevators. When the door closed he slipped a key into the panel, opening it, and pushed the button there.

Craig hadn't done that when she was here before but maybe security made evening access more intricate.

When the elevator stopped and opened its doors

Kelly was prepared to see his office lobby. Instead, she walked into another world.

The myriad of lights of Manhattan shone as far as she could see through floor-to-ceiling plate glass. Nick placed his hand in the small of her back and guided her around a corner to an equally fascinating view. A lovely table, complete with tapered candles and exquisite crystal and china, sat near the wall. The terrace that she could see through the glass wall was adorned with shrubs and flowers.

"You live here, don't you?" she demanded, knowing she'd been tricked.

He made a slight bow. "Yes."

"You could have at least given me a choice in the matter."

"And would you have come?" he asked, amusement lurking in his eyes.

"Of course not!"

"Which is why I chose to do it this way. Rest assured your virtue is completely safe."

A comfortably middle-aged woman came into the room. "Good evening," she said, smiling at them. "You must be Ms. MacLeod."

Nick turned to Kelly. "This is Andrea, Dimitrios's wife. They look after my home and keep my life on schedule."

"Dimitrios? Isn't he the one—"

"He's a world-class chef who does me the honor of working for me."

Andrea said, "We're ready to serve dinner at your convenience."

"Good. I'm starved." He glanced at Kelly. "Is that all right with you?"

Kelly could only nod. Her comfortable set of beliefs had just received a blow. Although she wasn't too surprised to find Nick living a posh, sequestered existence in his tower, discovering that he appeared to be on good terms with his employees seemed out of character...at least the character she had assigned to him. She supposed that even the most irredeemable villain had some good qualities.

He was probably kind to his mother.

Once they were seated and sipping delicious wine, Kelly ventured to ask, "You didn't inherit your present empire, did you?"

She watched the play of emotions across his face before he said, "No."

"You mentioned that you grew up in the Bronx. Do your parents still live there?"

He took his time answering. She thought he wasn't going to when he finally replied, "Like yours, both my parents are dead."

"Oh." She didn't want to think of him as a grieving son for some reason. When he offered nothing more, she finally asked, "Do you have brothers and sisters?"

"A brother. Loukas."

"He lives here?"

"No. He works overseas. He moves around a great deal. I rarely know where he is. He works for the government."

"Is he married?"

"Luke?" He shook his head. "He doesn't stay in

one place long enough to get seriously involved with anyone.''

At least he was answering her, though his reluctance was obvious. ''How did you manage to reach the pinnacle of success so young?''

His eyebrow arched. ''I'm not so young. I'm thirty-five.''

''Practically doddering,'' she quipped. ''What interested you in acquisitions?''

He frowned. ''Did I somehow give you the impression that this was a business dinner? If so, I want to disabuse you of that notion. In addition, I'd like to point out that I'm on my very best behavior, because at the moment all I can think about is how much I want to make love to you.''

Kelly swallowed, once again feeling out of her depth with this man. Not a pleasant feeling. ''Are you always so blunt?'' she asked, praying he didn't notice the tremor in her voice.

He took his time sipping his wine before he answered.

''Yes.''

She nodded. So much for her short-lived Mata Hari role. Even if she'd known the right questions to ask, he certainly wasn't volunteering any information.

Kelly concentrated on the meal, savoring each bit. Dimitrios performed magic in the kitchen, she had to admit.

After a lengthy silence, Nick said, ''Did I offend you with my honesty? If so, that wasn't my intention.''

''What are you trying to prove to me?''

"That I'm not the ogre you think I am," he promptly replied. "I was hoping that you would reserve further judgment of me until after we've had a chance to know each other better."

"Mmm," was all she could say in response. The image of a large, sleek tiger patiently waiting came to mind. If she continued to see him, she would be placing herself in the tiger's den. Not a particularly safe place to be...but there was no doubt being around Dominic Chakaris would be exciting.

"Your painting reveals that you've spent time studying me, so why shouldn't I have the opportunity to get to know you?"

"I'll give you that," she replied, feeling outmaneuvered. She returned to her meal and he took the hint, keeping the rest of their dinner conversation innocuous.

Once through with dinner, Nick suggested they have coffee on the terrace. He escorted her outside and they strolled to the waist-high wall near the edge. "This is beautiful," she said quietly.

"Yes," he replied, but when she glanced at him he wasn't looking at the view.

"Our being together would never work," she finally said, feeling far from relaxed but hoping her tension didn't show.

"Why not?"

"Because..." she paused, searching for words.

"Why don't we give it a try? What could it hurt?"

"What do you have in mind?" she asked cautiously.

For the first time since she'd met him he smiled. The smile transformed his austere face and made him devastatingly attractive.

"Not what you're thinking, obviously," he replied, his lips twitching. "I know I haven't hidden my desire for an intimate relationship with you. However, you're the one who will decide if and when that will happen."

"You're leaving the decision to me?"

"Absolutely."

She walked over to the wrought-iron table where Andrea had placed the tray of coffee, cups, cream and sugar and lowered herself onto a chaise lounge. She poured coffee for both of them and waited until he had sat on a chair nearby to hand him his coffee.

She had already discovered how he liked his coffee from their luncheon together. Funny she should remember that.

"I'm not afraid for my virtue, you know," she said and knew that wasn't true at all. She'd never felt such a strong sexual pull toward anyone before. Indeed, her virtue could very well be in jeopardy. However, that was a piece of information she chose not to share.

"What about Comstock?" he asked tersely.

"What about him?"

"Will you continue to see him as well?"

"Are you asking for an exclusive relationship?"

"Damn right I am and don't you forget it. You will receive the same from me. I'll admit that you're the one making most of the concessions because I travel a great deal. I may not always be available to escort you to every social event, but I'll do my best to be here whenever you've made plans.''

"I see. I'm supposed to sit home docilely until you have time for me, am I correct?''

"A less docile woman I've never met,'' he retorted. "Why don't we wait and see how it works out.''

She finished her coffee. "For some reason I feel as though our evening has indeed turned into a business meeting. Shouldn't I be signing some sort of contract or negotiating a fee schedule for this so-called relationship?''

He surged to his feet. "Is that what you think? That I'm such a bastard that I'd coldly arrange for you to be my mistress?'' He swung away from her, shoving his hand through his hair in agitation.

Amazing, she thought. For the first time since she'd met him, Kelly saw Nick lose his cool aloofness.

She stood and said, "I believe it's time for me to leave. Would you be so kind as to arrange a ride for me?''

His shoulders stiffened but he didn't say anything. When he did turn toward her, he looked perfectly composed. "Perhaps that would be a good idea,'' he agreed. "I'll call for the car.''

"You don't need to—''

He stopped her with a gesture. "Don't say any more. Please. Of course I'll take you home. I know that you want to assert your independence where I'm concerned. Consider it done.''

They were silent on the way back to her home. When he helped her out of the limousine and walked her to her door, she said, "You were right. Dimitrios is a jewel. The meal was spectacular." She removed her keys from her purse and turned to Nick. "Thank you for the evening." She held out her hand to him.

Nick glanced down at her hand, took it and pulled her to him. Without pausing he drew her into his arms and kissed her. Not fair, she thought wildly, not fair at all. Because the man knew how to kiss.

That was the last coherent thought she had as his lips softened and shaped themselves to hers. He tilted her head back with his thumb before he drew his tongue across her lips. She opened to him and steadied herself with her hands on his chest as though to withstand a tidal wave.

She had no idea how long they stood there, kissing, reluctantly drawing away from each other only to come together again.

When Nick finally let go of her, he moved an arm's length away. His lips tilted into a half smile. "If there was ever any doubt that we would be compatible in bed, I believe we've dispelled it. Good night, Kelly. Sleep well."

Kelly was up early Monday, ready to get to work. She headed toward the kitchen. Bridget generally set out a basket of croissants, a variety of fruit and hot coffee so that Kelly could eat whenever she wished. This morning she was grateful for the privacy.

She'd looked into the mirror this morning and was appalled at how pale she looked. The only color there was in the shadows beneath her eyes. Her fair skin was one of the downsides of being a natural blonde…that and having to listen to dumb-blonde jokes.

Since meeting Nick last week, she hadn't had a decent night's sleep. Another mark against the man.

She poured her coffee, filled a plate with fruit and a croissant and took the plate and coffee up to her studio. This room was her sanctuary…her retreat…her place to think clearly.

The first thing she saw when she walked through the door was the painting of Nick that had arrived Saturday. Placing it where she could see it first thing this morning certainly brought her sense of self-preservation into question.

Kelly wandered over to the portrait and studied it while she drank her coffee. How arrogant of her to think she could paint a person she didn't really know.

She still considered the man ruthless. He made no excuse for who he was and the painting clearly captured that part of him. She needed to keep that fact in mind.

Kelly sat and stared at the painting while she finished her breakfast, then turned the painting toward the wall so she wouldn't be further distracted.

Once focused on her current project, Kelly managed to make good progress. By noon she had finished her commission for Mrs. Gregory Bernhardt, whose husband was involved in international banking.

Kelly had done some judicious thinning of Mrs. Bernhardt's jowls in an effort to make the woman look less like a bulldog. There was nothing she could do about her close-set eyes and supercilious smile.

She stepped back and studied the finished product while she cleaned her brushes. When had most of her work in the past few years evolved into painting bored women with too much time and money on their hands?

She thought of Italy and how much she had loved the light there…and the countryside…the picturesque buildings…the sea. Maybe she would go there for a while and paint whatever happened to appeal to her. She definitely needed a break.

She peeked into the kitchen and said, "I'm starved, Bridget. What's for lunch?"

Bridget turned from her work at the counter and said, "Your lunch is in the refrigerator. Help yourself."

Kelly looked inside and found a large salad with slivers of meat on top of luscious fresh vegetables. She bumped her hip against the door to close it and started into the dining room. Tucked into a corner was a small table where she generally had her meals.

"Oh, I almost forgot," Bridget said as Kelly started through the doorway, "Mr. Lancaster called. He said to call him at your convenience."

"Thanks," Kelly said, continuing into the dining room. She set her food on the table. Bridget brought her iced tea and returned to the kitchen.

George Lancaster had been the family attorney for as long as she could remember. He was her father's age, somewhere in his mid-sixties, and had retired a couple of years ago. When her mother died, Kelly had asked him if he would handle the estate, which he'd been willing to do.

As soon as she had finished eating, Kelly went back upstairs and called him from her workroom phone.

"Hello, George," she said when he answered. "You wanted me to call you?"

"Ah, yes. How are things going for you these days?"

"I'm keeping busy."

He chuckled. "I would certainly agree with that."

"What do you mean?"

"There was a lovely photo of you in the paper this morning. You and your date seemed to be enthralled with each other."

"What?!"

"I thought you would have already seen it."

"No. I usually wait 'til afternoon to read the paper." How had someone gotten her picture? And with whom? And why would she be considered news?

"I wasn't aware that you and Dominic Chakaris were such good friends."

Ah. Nick. The answer to two of her questions.

"We've just met, actually. I don't know him very well."

George laughed. "You certainly couldn't prove it by looking at the photo."

Her heart sank.

"That isn't the reason I called, by the way."

"Oh."

"I'm having trouble with one of the insurance companies. Their policy wasn't in the group you gave me so I was unaware of its existence until a week ago when I happened to run across a notation in one of the family files. The insurance company insists on having a copy of the policy. There was a merger of that company with another a few years ago and I guess some of their records were lost, so it's imperative we find it. I was wondering if you might know where it is?''

''Not really. I went through all of the papers my dad left in his desk after he died and gave you everything I'd found at that time.''

''Perhaps your mother kept it somewhere.''

''That's a possibility. If so, it's in her desk in her bedroom. I've just begun sorting through her things. So far, I've only sorted through her dressing room.''

''See what you can do, okay?''

''Certainly. I'll go look right now.''

He gave her the name of the insurance company and hung up.

Kelly dutifully wrote down the information although her mind was far from what she was doing. As soon as she replaced the phone she raced downstairs to the den where Bridget left mail, magazines and newspapers.

She spread the morning paper open on the desk and scanned each page, coming to an abrupt halt at the front page of the lifestyle section. Whoever took the photograph was outside her home when she and Nick arrived. What a creepy thought that was.

The photo had been taken of her front door with a zoom lens.

She and Nick were leaning toward each her, his hand on hers, their gazes locked. Anyone seeing it could easily conclude the shared look was one of passion.

What if there were other photos? Of that kiss that had caused her brain to numb out, for instance?

Kelly groaned and sat back in her chair. Great. Nothing like adding more complications to an already complex situation.

Technology had certainly come a long way. The photograph, taken without a flash, was sharp and clear. Despite being black and white, the setting and the subjects were easily identifiable.

Damn.

Kelly sighed and got up. George needed her to find that policy. Sitting here staring at the paper wasn't going to get that done.

She went upstairs to her mother's room and looked around.

There were several drawers where the policy could be kept—the bedside table, the highboy, the dresser—but she hoped she would find it in her mother's desk. She would start looking there.

Kelly had just sat down at the desk when the phone rang. "Hello?"

"We made the papers," a deep voice said cheerfully.

"So we did," she replied coolly.

"You know what this means, don't you?"

"You tell me," she suggested warily.

He chuckled. He actually sounded pleased. About

what? It couldn't be the photograph. Could it? "We are now officially an item," he replied.

"Would it do any good to deny it?"

"Never deny anything. It's a waste of time since no one will believe you anyway." He paused before saying, "Besides, why deny something that could turn into truth. Stranger things have happened, you know. I believe we should spend this evening together...go dancing, perhaps. Plus I have tickets for the orchestra on Wednesday."

Her knee-jerk reaction was to tell him no. She wasn't ready to expose herself to more of his rather lethal charm so soon after the weekend.

"I'm afraid I have other plans tonight," she finally replied.

"Oh?" he replied, sounding skeptical.

She owed him no explanation for not going with him. "As for Wednesday," she said thoughtfully, "I enjoy the orchestra."

"With dinner afterward?"

"That's a little late for me."

"Than I'll pick you up in time to eat before we go. About six, say?"

"All right."

"Have fun tonight," he said softly.

"I intend to," she replied.

They hung up and Kelly sat staring at the phone. She couldn't believe she'd accepted another date with him. Obviously her willpower where he was concerned needed shoring up.

She turned to the desk and concentrated on finding

the insurance policy for George. When she stopped looking late that afternoon, she had exhausted her list of places to search.

While she showered and dressed to meet a couple of friends, Kelly thought about other places she might look. Her mother's desk had revealed very little besides stationery, pens and stamps…nothing that resembled legal papers.

Oh, well. She'd forget about it for now and continue the search tomorrow.

The phone rang a little after eleven that night. Kelly was in bed reading. Who would call at this time of night? She was tempted to allow the answering machine to pick up until her curiosity got the best of her.

She picked up the phone and held it to her ear without speaking.

"Kelly?" Nick said.

"Yes?"

"Did I wake you?"

"No."

"How was your evening?"

"Enjoyable."

"Will we see another picture of you in tomorrow's paper?"

She thought about the pizza place where she and her two girlfriends had gone after seeing a three-hankie movie. "Somehow I doubt it," she said, smiling.

"I was ready to go home when I thought I'd call to let you know I was thinking of you."

"You're still at your office?"

"Yes."

"Do you usually work such late hours?"

"Only when I can't convince you to go to dinner with me, thus saving me from the life of a workaholic."

She shook her head. He had an answer for everything.

Curious, she asked, "Do you ever take a vacation?"

"Not so far."

"Perhaps you should consider it some time," she replied.

"Only if you'll come with me."

"You know better than that," she chided him.

"What did I say? Going away with me doesn't automatically mean sleeping with me, you know."

"Really?" she replied doubtfully.

"Making slow, passionate love to you isn't the only reason I want to spend time with you. I enjoy your company, Kelly. I find you very restful to be around."

"I wish you would tell my friends that. Restful isn't the first trait they mention when they talk about me. I doubt they would recognize your description of me."

"I'll let you go to sleep. Dream of me," he said, a suggestion she found outrageous.

The problem was, she probably would.

Chapter Six

Kelly was dismayed to discover that she was looking forward to seeing Nick Wednesday evening. It was true she enjoyed going to hear the orchestra and she hadn't been in a while, but it was the idea of spending time with Nick that made her feel flushed and nervous, as though she were a teenager going on her first date.

As soon as he arrived her heart began beating in double time.

She took a deep, calming breath as she let him inside. "Would you like a glass of wine before we leave?" she asked.

"Yes, thank you. This is the first time I've been in your home. It's quite lovely."

They walked into the living room. Since Kelly had grown up with the lovely furniture and furnishings, including the original oils hanging on the walls, she tended to take her home for granted.

She poured them each a glass of wine and sat down in a delicate, straight-backed chair. Kelly noticed that Nick seemed to take over a room simply by walking into it.

He sat on the love seat across from her. "You're looking stunning, as usual," he said. "I've seen you in gold, in black and now in green. I can't decide what color I like best on you." He took a sip. "Of course, I also visualize you wearing little more than a sheet, as well."

She chuckled. "I believe you say things like that just to see what my reaction will be."

"And?"

Honesty compelled her to reply, "Let's just say your comments certainly get my attention."

He'd been lounging in the corner of the love seat until she spoke. Then, he sat up and leaned forward, his elbows on his knees. "There are so many traits about you that I admire. You fascinate me." He shook his head ruefully. "I may have been joking at first about your distracting me but I discovered that it was the truth. In a meeting yesterday I kept drifting off and I'd find myself thinking of you rather than paying attention to the meeting. I can't remember ever being quite this distracted."

"I think it's time to go, don't you?" she asked smoothly.

"I apologize if I've offended you. It's just that you're so different from most women I know. You're not at all jaded in your outlook. You're far from being a bored former debutante.'' He shook his head. ''I sound ridiculous even to myself. You're right. We need to go.''

Bridget appeared in the foyer as they were about to leave. ''Bridget, this is Dominic Chakaris.''

Before she could continue with the introductions, Bridget calmly said, ''I recognize you from the painting.''

He nodded. ''Yes, I've been told Kelly's rendition of me is strikingly accurate.'' He glanced at Kelly, who continued the introductions.

''Bridget has been our housekeeper for as far back as I can remember. I don't think I could function without her.'' To Bridget she said, ''No need to wait up for me tonight. I'll see you in the morning.''

On the way to the restaurant, he said, ''If I promise not to say anything personal about you, will you stop pressing against the car door and move closer to me?''

''I'm far from the door, Nick. This car is so large you could carry a basketball team in here with plenty of room.''

Kelly edged closer to Nick, who immediately took her hand and placed it on his black-clad knee. ''You have such delicate hands,'' he said softly, tracing her fingers with one of his own.

''My size was the bane of my existence as a child. I was always being teased and accused of being in the wrong classroom.''

''There's no mistaking you for a schoolgirl now. Have you always wanted to be an artist?'' he asked, deflecting any comment she might make about the personal nature of his remarks.

"I think I must have been drawing with the first pencil I found. My parents always encouraged me to pursue my dreams. They remodeled one of the rooms upstairs into a studio for me when I was twelve."

Nick didn't want to ask questions about her parents and remind her that she held him responsible for her loss. However, he was curious to learn everything he could about her. He was amused to realize that he was approaching this relationship much as he did the acquisition of a business. He wanted to get to know her...but not for a business reason.

She intrigued him.

The restaurant he'd chosen was well known for its excellent cuisine and quiet atmosphere. Once they stepped out of the limo at the canopied entrance, though, they were rushed by a couple of photographers who began to snap their pictures.

"Ignore them," he said into her ear.

"Since every flash blinds me, I'm finding that difficult to do. Do they follow you around?"

"No. The freelancers know several places around town where people of interest can generally be found, so they wait for someone to come along. Tonight must be a slow night for them to be wasting film on me."

The maître d' was waiting by the front door and immediately spotted them as they stepped inside. "Good evening, Mr. Chakaris. It's good to see you again." He led the way to a secluded corner of the room.

The waiter appeared immediately and took their drink orders. They studied the menu, discussed various options and when the waiter returned, Nick gave him their selections.

Once the waiter had left, Kelly said, "How did the photographer get our picture Sunday evening? My home is certainly not a hangout for celebrities."

"Actually, I wondered the same thing. He could have spotted us leaving my building and followed us, I suppose. He must have been desperate for something to sell."

"If he got the one of our standing there, it's my guess he took more, including our kiss."

He grinned, looking boyish. "That's a thought. Maybe I'll buy one of them, myself."

"You really don't mind being the object of so much publicity, do you?"

"Yes, I do mind. However, I learned at an early age not to fret about things I can't change. To some publications, I'm news of a sort. I can't change that. As long as they continue to purchase photos from freelance photographers, there's nothing to be done. Eventually something newsworthy will happen and I'll be relegated back to obscurity again, which is my preference."

"I've never dated someone like you."

"What do you mean?"

"Your attitude toward life, I suppose. Your blunt manner. It's difficult for me to see what you could possibly find interesting in me. Or is it the chase that excites you?"

Nick took his time answering her. After he sipped his wine, he said, "You know, Kelly, you manage to insult me so casually that it takes a split-second for me to actually feel the knife inserted between my shoulder blades." He studied her for a moment. "I believe I've made it clear why I'm pursuing you...and it isn't because of the thrill of the chase, as you put it."

The waiter returned with their salads and it was then Kelly noticed that several people at other tables were gazing at them. From their expressions, she gathered that they were attempting to figure out who she was.

If she wanted to keep a low profile, dating Nick wasn't the way to do it.

Later, during the symphony, Nick sat next to Kelly in their box watching her. She was absorbed in the music, oblivious to everyone around her. He actually envied the orchestra their hold on her senses.

You've got it bad, he thought. He wanted to become a part of her daily life. With his schedule, though, he wasn't certain quite how he was going to manage that. There was always the telephone, he supposed.

By the time they reached Kelly's home, Nick, like a randy teenager, had to fight his desire to wrap his arms around her and not let her go. He walked her to the door and was surprised when she said, "Would you like to come in?"

"All right, thank you." Nick was pleased that he could sound so casual.

"Coffee?" she asked after leading him to a library/ den located beyond the foyer.

Nick walked over to some bookshelves. "Sounds good." He forced himself not to watch her leave the room. He scanned titles, impressed by the varied subjects and the extensive collection of Elizabethan literature.

He wished he'd known Kelly's father better. He scarcely remembered their final meeting. Nick could appreciate the man's wide range of knowledge despite the fact he hadn't been a very astute businessman.

He turned at the slight sound of Kelly's step several minutes later and strode across the room to take the tray she was carrying from her. Once seated, they looked at each other.

Kelly felt awkward, which was absurd. "I thought the orchestra surpassed itself tonight," she finally said.

"Mmm."

"Did you enjoy it?"

"Yes," he replied crisply.

Kelly wondered what was wrong with him. He'd become increasingly quiet as the evening progressed. Now he looked positively grim.

"Is the coffee all right?" she asked.

He nodded. "Yes." He finished the coffee in his cup and said abruptly, "I need to go."

Kelly couldn't believe she felt a pan of regret—slight though it might be—at his words. "Of course," she said, standing when he did. She walked him to the door.

He turned and looked at her. "When can I see you again?"

"When would you like to see me again?" she asked softly.

"Soon, whenever you're available."

There was no reason to be coy. She disliked women who were. "I don't have anything planned for the weekend."

"Good. Consider the weekend booked."

She blinked. "All of it?"

He nodded and placed his hands on her shoulders. "I'll call you tomorrow," he said, giving her a light kiss on the mouth.

At least the kiss began as a light, friendly expression of affection. Kelly took a step closer and kissed him back, feeling safe from things going too far while they stood in the foyer.

He deepened the kiss and she relaxed into his arms, feeling his heart thundering against her breast. When he nudged her mouth with his tongue, she opened to him, drowning in sensation.

Oh, yes, this man was dangerous. If she'd had any doubt before, it was gone now. She teased him with her tongue, imitating his movements. For such a hard man, mentally and physically, his lips were surprisingly soft and seductive.

Finally, he stepped away from her with a moan. "If I don't leave right now, I won't be leaving at all."

Kelly grabbed the door and opened it before she impulsively asked him to stay. She reminded herself that she wasn't going to be seduced by this man. Despite her shaking knees, she managed to say, "Thank you for the evening, Nick. I enjoyed it.'' She sounded breathless. Hopefully he hadn't noticed.

He looked at her with the same grim expression she'd seen earlier and said, ''I'll call you.'' He walked out the door without looking back.

As soon as she closed and locked the door, Kelly fanned herself. Whew, could that man kiss! He had her so hot and bothered she wasn't certain she'd be able to sleep.

With something close to a smile she realized that she would spend another sleepless night because of Nick.

Once in bed, she attempted to read but couldn't concentrate. When the phone rang, she was glad for the interruption…until she heard Nick's voice. ''I didn't realize you meant you'd call tonight,'' she said.

''I wanted to talk to you about the weekend except I find you so distracting in person I have trouble concentrating.''

It was good to know she wasn't the only one with that problem. ''Okay,'' she finally replied.

''Be ready at three on Friday with enough clothes for the weekend.''

''Why?''

''I thought we might drive up to New England and enjoy the fall foliage.''

''In a limo?''

''No. I have a two-seater convertible.''

''Only if it's clear to you that I don't intend to share a bed with you.''

There was only a slight pause before he said, "Agreed. Sleep well. I'll see you Friday."

As usual Nick was prompt. At three o'clock on Friday the doorbell rang. Kelly had repacked her small weekend bag so many times her clothes probably showed the wear and tear of being handled so much. Since she'd never done anything like this before, she wasn't certain of the protocol. She wanted to give the impression that their trip wasn't anything unusual for her and hoped the clothes she'd finally chosen would help to do that.

She went to the door and called, "I'm leaving, Bridget. I'll see you Sunday."

"Be careful," Bridget called and Kelly smiled. Very good advice, indeed.

She opened the door to Nick. He stood there waiting. "Hello, Nick," she said, stepping outside with her bag. He took it from her without a word and turned to the street.

His hair looked mussed. He wore a sports jacket and slacks rather than a suit. Somehow she always pictured him in her mind in a tuxedo or custom-made suits. This Nick looked much more approachable...which might not be such a good thing if she intended to maintain her emotional distance from him.

Kelly looked past him and smiled. He had the top down on his BMW. No wonder his hair looked rumpled. She'd brought one of her small-brimmed hats to pull over her hair. She saw no reason to have her hair whipping her for the duration of their trip.

Still silent, Nick opened the door for her before

placing her bag in the trunk of the car. Once inside, Nick pulled smoothly out in the traffic, drumming his fingers lightly on the wheel.

Ten minutes later she said, "Have you taken a vow of silence for the weekend?" she asked.

He glanced at her and shook his head. "I've got a lot on my mind at the moment."

She nodded in understanding. "Of course. You're trying to decide on the next business you want to rape and pillage."

"How astute of you. That's exactly what I was thinking."

Actually, Nick had probably blown a deal he'd been working on for months by canceling his plans to fly to San Francisco for a meeting scheduled for tomorrow. When he looked at his schedule yesterday and realized he'd forgotten the meeting, which was the culmination of laborious negotiations, he'd reached for the phone to call Kelly.

However, when he had the phone in his hand he called San Francisco instead. He told the head of the company that a family emergency had come up and he wouldn't be able to come. He promised to get in touch with them to set up another meeting.

When he'd told Craig what he'd done, Craig had said nothing. He'd shaken his head and muttered something inaudible. Nick hadn't asked him to repeat it.

He glanced at Kelly again. She looked adorable with a hat framing her face. She hadn't said a word about the open car, gamely pulling on the hat when he started the car.

He didn't care what Craig thought—he needed some time off. He'd kept a hectic pace for years without giving his schedule much thought. Staying busy was what he needed to do in order to get where he wanted to go. Somewhere along the way, though, he'd lost sight of the goal. Hell, he hadn't even celebrated when he'd made his first million...or his second...or the many after that.

This trip with Kelly was a gift he'd given himself and he was determined to enjoy it.

"I'm sorry," he finally said.

"For what?"

"Ignoring you. I've been looking forward to this weekend and now that we're underway I'm off somewhere else."

"I'm surprised you had the time to get away."

"It took some doing, I'll admit."

With the tension eased between them they chatted about the traffic and the route he'd chosen to take. They stopped at a picturesque inn for a leisurely and elegant dinner. It was late when they pulled into the driveway of a hotel. "I made reservations here because I've stayed here before. From now on, though, we'll go where we want, and take what we can get for amenities."

She looked at him with a smile. "Yes, but I understand that civilization has managed to catch on here in Connecticut. We probably won't have to chop wood, carry water or pitch a tent."

"You like to make fun of me, don't you?" he said, stopping in front of the hotel entrance.

"I confess I do. Why?"

He shrugged. "I'm not used to anyone—outside of Craig—giving me a bad time. It startles me sometimes when you do it."

"Consider it one of my more endearing qualities."

He got out of the car. "I'll be right back. Don't go away."

"You needn't worry since you took the keys with you."

He smiled. "Force of habit." She noticed that he didn't offer them to her, however.

Kelly watched him walk through the revolving doors. There was something about the way he walked that she found eye-catching. She had no idea why. His no-nonsense stride mirrored his personality, she supposed. What surprised her was that she liked his personality. Who would have guessed?

Before long he returned, tossed two small folders in her lap and drove the car into the parking lot. After he raised the top and removed their bags, he set his alarm and turned to her. "Those contain our room keys. You can take your pick. I would imagine the rooms are just alike."

He led the way back to the lobby and the elevators. They stepped out on the third floor. He checked the numbers with the arrow signs on the wall and turned down one of the hallways. Halfway to the end, he stopped, placed their bags on the floor, and held out his hand.

She gave him both folders. He pulled out the plastic card in one of them and opened the door. He picked up her bag and motioned for her to go inside.

The room was quite nice. When she turned back to Nick, he'd put her bag on the bed. "Call me when you're ready for breakfast." He gave her the other folder after removing the plastic card in there. "This is the number of my room."

With that said, Nick walked out of the room and quietly closed the door.

Kelly pulled off her hat and ran her fingers through her hair. Well. That was interesting. She wasn't sure what she had expected from their first night together but his brusque manner surprised her. She wondered if he already regretted their trip.

She shrugged. She might as well make the best of it. With that resolve, Kelly went in to the bathroom to take her shower and get ready for bed.

Nick walked into his room, which was down the hall from Kelly's and immediately went into the bathroom to take a shower...a very cold shower. Was he going to spend the rest of the weekend in this semi-aroused state? he wondered. He sincerely hoped not.

He wanted to make love to her and his body kept reminding him of that fact. Somehow he had to relax and enjoy Kelly's companionship without expectations of more. If it weren't so painful he'd find it amusing to be faced with the present situation. Many of the women he knew made it clear they were available. The few times he'd taken one of them up on her offer he'd ended their first evening together in bed.

He couldn't remember the last time he'd pursued anyone, for the simple reason that he didn't have time. Yet, here he was, pursuing Kelly and attempting to convince his body that he was going to bed alone, despite being with her all day.

Nick woke early the next morning as usual and for a moment thought he was somewhere out of town for a meeting. A glance around the room dispelled that notion. He saw no briefcase, no stack of papers, nothing to indicate this was a business trip.

He smiled. Kelly was just down the hall and all was right with his world.

When Kelly woke, sunshine was filtering through the sheers at the window, touching each object in the room with gold. She dressed and called Nick. He answered on the second ring by saying, "Good morning. I hope you slept well."

Okay, so she was the only one who knew where he was but his cheerful response startled her.

"I seem to have overslept," she said.

"Are you ready for breakfast?"

"Sounds wonderful."

"I'll be right there."

She was left holding the phone. Did he have to be quite so abrupt? It seemed to be a habit of his. When Kelly opened the door he was a couple of yards away. She stepped out into the hall and closed her door.

Nick looked more rested than she'd ever seen him.

The lines around his eyes were gone. He kissed her lightly, startling her, and said, "I'm starved." He took her hand and they walked to the elevator.

After giving their orders to the waitress in the hotel coffee shop, Kelly said, "Something's different about you today. I can't quite decide what it is."

He gave her a lopsided smile. "I woke up at my usual time this morning, realized there was no reason to get up, rolled over and went back to sleep."

"Good for you."

A mischievous glint appeared in his eyes. "If you had been in bed with me, I'm sure I could have thought of something to do."

She shook her head and smiled at him. "You have sex on the brain."

Her words seemed to startle him. After a moment, "I suppose you're right, but only since I met you."

"I'm no femme fatale."

"Strange, isn't it," he mused, "that I only realized that now."

"That I'm no femme fatale?" she asked, smiling at him.

"No, that you have this ability to keep my thoughts on—uh—well, never mind."

Kelly didn't quite know what to make of his comment. She knew of a few women in her social circle who had relentlessly pursued Nick. If he dated any of them, it was never apparent. One had later muttered that he was a cold fish who seemed uninterested in anything but business.

He seemed anything but a cold fish to her.

By the time Nick dropped her off at home on Sunday afternoon, Kelly had a new perspective on the man. He had been friendly during their drive. He hadn't talked much, but that wasn't unusual. They had ridden along with the top down in companionable silence, enjoying the beautiful autumn foliage. They had chatted over their meals and spent Saturday night at a quaint inn. She almost laughed at the look on the clerk's face when Nick asked for two rooms.

All right. He had shown her a different side of him, but she reminded herself that his goal was to change her opinion of him and he'd been diligent in his efforts. She wondered if he knew how persuasive and charming he was when he tried.

Of course he did. And it had worked to some degree. She no longer despised him.

He'd been a gentleman during their time together, if she discounted all the blatant sexual comments he made. Perhaps she should have been shocked and insulted. Instead, she'd been amused and intrigued. She had no intention of having an affair with him, of course. That would be foolish in the extreme. When he called the next time, she wouldn't let this past weekend influence her feelings. She needed to keep her distance or there was a real likelihood that she could get hurt.

Chapter Seven

"You appear in fine spirits this morning," Craig said on Monday when Nick arrived ten minutes late for their regular morning meeting with a scowl on his face.

"Then looks are deceiving," Nick replied, tossing the suit coat he'd draped over one shoulder onto a chair. "I've been looking at my schedule." He tossed his calendar in front of Craig. "Would you look at that?"

Puzzled, Craig said, "I see it. I just don't know what the problem is. It looks like it always has."

"I'm booked all day every day and most weekends for the next three months! I had to cancel my San Francisco trip to get the past two days off!"

"Uh-huh," Craig replied slowly. "And your point is?"

"When am I going to have time for some kind of social life?"

Craig's eyebrows climbed. "Are we by chance talking about Ms. MacLeod?"

"*I'm* not, even though you may be. I'm just saying that if I would like to take, say, a week off, I would have to plan months in advance!"

"So you would. And for whatever reason, this has only now become clear to you. Interesting."

"Never mind," Nick said, sounding disgruntled. "Have you spoken to the accountants about the San Francisco deal?"

Craig laughed. "Yes. The figures are right here. I'm disappointed, though. I thought we were going to discuss your personal life."

"That will never happen," Nick snapped. "Let's go over the agenda for the ten o'clock meeting."

Kelly woke up Monday morning trying to figure out where the missing insurance policy might be. She reviewed every place she had looked, puzzled that the policy hadn't been with the rest of the papers. Her father had always been meticulous about keeping his papers organized.

Over breakfast she mulled over other possibilities. The only other place she could think to look was the attic. There was no reason to think it would be up there, but she had run out of ideas. If she didn't find it up there, she'd have to let George know that if the policy had existed at one time, there was no sign of it now.

According to George's file, the policy had been purchased twenty-five years ago, not long after she'd been
born. Perhaps her mother had mistakenly put the policy in one of the files that had been stored in the attic
instead of in the safe with the rest of the family papers.

Covering her hair with a kerchief and donning an
old beach cover-up to stay as clean as possible, Kelly
headed for the attic immediately after breakfast.

Not for the first time in the past year, she wished
her mother were there. She still missed her so much.
Kelly had always been able to share any of her cares
or concerns with her mother, whose wise advice had
always helped Kelly look at whatever was bothering
her with a new perspective.

She wished she could talk to her mother about the
present situation with Nick. Kelly was confused by her
conflicting emotions where Nick was concerned. She
wondered what sort of advice her mother might have
given her. Would she have told her to let go of the
past, which couldn't be changed? Or would she see
Kelly's association with Nick as a betrayal of the family?

Kelly thought back to the times when her mother
had advised her and, for the first time, realized that
her mother had never blamed anyone for the loss of
the family business. She had said more than once that
things generally worked out for the best in the long
run. For that matter, Kelly had never heard her mother
make an unkind remark about anyone.

She had a hunch that her mother would have liked
Nick. His drive and determination would have im-

pressed her and as far as her mother was concerned, anyone who admired Kelly obviously had excellent taste.

Kelly smiled at the thought, almost hearing her mother's voice.

Once in the attic, Kelly turned in a slow circle, trying to decide where to begin. In her mother's usual tidy manner, she'd labeled and arranged everything up there.

Kelly couldn't remember having been in the attic in years. Who knew what family information she could find if she wanted to take the time to search. At the moment, though, she would be grateful to locate the insurance policy in question.

She came across file boxes stacked and labeled by year. That was certainly going to help. She searched for the year the policy had been issued. For some reason that box had been set aside from the others, as though discarded. Not a good sign.

She dragged the box over by a window to see what she could find.

It was crammed full of papers, so maybe there was hope. She slowly scanned every paper in each file in case the policy had been misfiled.

She had just about given up when she found it near the back of the box. Thank God. Feeling considerably lighter, Kelly began to replace the files she'd pulled out only to pause when she saw a large brown envelope that had slipped down into the bottom of the storage box.

She picked it up. The legal-size envelope was yellowed with age, but no more so than most of the papers filed there.

The return address was from solicitors in Scotland. Her mother had never mentioned knowing anyone in Scotland. Perhaps it had something to do with some genealogical research her mother had pursued. Kelly might find out something about their Scottish ancestors.

How exciting.

Kelly gathered up her finds, finished repacking everything else she'd taken out of the box and went downstairs.

Despite all her gallant efforts, she was grimy with dust. She tossed the policy and the envelope on her bed and took a shower.

Afterwards, Kelly took the papers downstairs to the den where she intended to call George with the good news. With a great deal of anticipation Kelly picked up the envelope from Scotland.

The envelope was addressed to Mr. and Mrs. Kevin MacLeod. The postage date was a few months after she'd been born. She smiled. Perhaps her birth had started her mother on an ancestral search.

Angus MacLeod had come to America from Glasgow. The solicitors' address was in Edinburgh. She loved a good mystery, and tracing the family tree would be great fun. She wished she'd learned about this years ago.

Kelly carefully opened the envelope and pulled out papers fragile with age.

The first thing she noticed was that the document

had nothing to do with family history. She stared at it, puzzled. Calvin McCloskey, a solicitor, had mailed adoption papers.

Adoption papers? Mailed to her parents? Had they tried to adopt after she was born and hadn't been able to do so?

She continued to read, more curious than concerned.

Until the papers stated that the child was a girl born on September 28, 1978.

Her birthday.

She suddenly felt cold. What was this? She quickly read through the rest of the documents. Clipped on the last page was a form that had been filled in by hand. It gave vital statistics of a live birth and was signed by the attending physician, a Dr. James MacDonald.

She dropped the papers as though they'd burned her fingers. What was this all about? According to these papers, she was adopted. She hadn't been born in New York as she'd been told all of her life, but in Scotland.

Kelly jumped to her feet and went to the wall safe. With trembling hands, she carefully worked the combination until the safe opened. She pulled out various documents until she found the one she wanted—her birth certificate.

She sat at the desk and placed the certificates side by side. Instead of Baby Girl for the name, the New York document listed her name. It showed that she had been born at home...and delivered by Dr. James MacDonald.

She tried to think but all she could do was feel. Her head felt as though it were bursting. This wasn't some oversight on the part of her parents. They had deliberately made her believe she'd been born to them. She had albums full of photos they had taken of her from the time she was only a few weeks old, with either one or both of her parents beaming with pride in each picture.

They hadn't intended for her to find out, obviously. If she hadn't been looking for that policy, there was a good chance she never would have.

If she wasn't the daughter of Kevin and Grace MacLeod, then who was she?

She knew enough to recognize that she had gone into shock. Rubbing her head, she tried to think. She needed a cup of tea...tea with sugar. She focused on walking to the kitchen, moving as though she were in pain.

While she waited for the water to boil, Kelly stood by the stove and stared blankly out the window. Bridget walked into the kitchen and stopped when she saw Kelly.

"Did you find it?" she asked, walking over to the stove where the water was beginning to boil. She saw the tea bag and sugar bowl, mute evidence of Kelly's intentions, and finished making the tea.

"Find what?" Kelly asked, her mind muddled.

Bridget looked at her. "Why, the policy, of course. Isn't that what you've been turning the place upside down for?"

"Oh. Yes. I found it."

Bridget put the cup on the kitchen table and stared

at Kelly in confusion. "Here. Sit. You wanted tea, didn't you?"

Like an automaton, Kelly stumbled to the table and lowered herself into the chair. She used both hands to pick up the cup, her hands shaking so she was afraid the hot liquid would spill.

"You look like you saw a ghost," Bridget said, looking more closely at her. "Are you all right?"

Instead of answering, Kelly asked, "How long have you worked for my family?"

Bridget sat across from Kelly, frowning. "Strange thing to be asking me at this late date. Most of my life, it seems," she replied. "Why?"

"Were you here when I was born?"

Bridget smiled. "I'm afraid I missed that blessed event. You were a tiny thing when your family hired me. Your parents explained they had been away on an extended trip and had dismissed the help. When they returned, your mother had hired a new staff. I was one of them, for which I'm thankful. Why do you ask?"

Kelly sipped tea until she felt she could speak without tearing up. "Did my parents ever mention to you that I was adopted?"

"Adopted! Why, of course not! Why would they tell such a tale?"

"Because I was. I just found the papers that prove I was born in Scotland and adopted by them."

"But how could that be? Your mother said you were born in New York. I believe your birth certificate says so."

"It seems they lied about that as well as everything else. My entire life appears to be a colossal lie."

"I'm shocked to hear this, Kelly…as you must be. No wonder you look close to fainting. Here, let me get you more tea. This time I'll double the sugar." Bridget muttered to herself as she filled the cup, "Of all things! There was never a hint. I'm having trouble taking this all in myself. I can only imagine what you must be feeling."

"I feel a little better, knowing I wasn't the only one who was kept in the dark," Kelly said, accepting the refilled cup.

Bridget poured herself one. "I don't know what to say." She was quiet for a few minutes, then added, "Not that it changes who you are, you know. I never knew two people who loved a child more, that's for sure."

Kelly nodded. "I used to ask why I didn't have a brother or sister and they would make up some teasing answer. As I grew older I stopped asking. This explains why I'm an only child."

"I know you're upset, them keeping this a secret from you and everything, but maybe you'll find it in your heart to forgive them. I'm sure they meant well."

"But who were they protecting?"

"What do you mean?"

"They hid a fundamental fact about my existence from me. Was it to protect me or to protect my birth parents?"

Bridget reached over and patted Kelly's hand.

"Whatever their reason, you can be assured of one thing—they did it out of love for you."

Kelly went to her room and fell across the bed, reviewing her life through a new filter.

Of course Bridget was right. Her new knowledge didn't change anything and yet it changed everything. It changed how she saw herself. It changed who she was. What was wrong with her that her parents—her adoptive parents, she mentally corrected herself—wouldn't or couldn't tell her about herself and her background?

How would she ever find out?

She closed her eyes as memories drifted through her mind.

She remembered her father, reluctantly going to the factory, telling her he would much prefer to stay home and play with her.

These people had loved her; there was no question about that. They had also lied to her and this was what she had trouble grasping. Why keep it such a secret?

Was it because of her real parents? She wondered who they might be and how she could find out more about them. All she had to go on were the names of the attending doctor and the solicitor in Edinburgh.

Was the firm still in existence after all these years?

Was there any way she could find out?

She dozed, her mind's way of sheltering her while she adjusted to her recent shock. When she roused some time later, she knew what she had to do.

She called George.

As soon as he answered, she said, "George," then had to stop. Hearing his voice triggered an emotional response in her she hadn't expected. She wept silently.

"I hope you're calling to say you found that policy," he said cheerfully.

She swallowed. "Yes, as a matter of fact, I did," she managed to get out.

"Kelly? Are you all right?"

She shook her head despite the fact he couldn't see her. "I need to talk with you," she said, her voice quivering.

"That's what you're doing. Tell me what's wrong."

Haltingly, she repeated to him all that had happened that afternoon. When she finished, George didn't respond right away.

"Well, I'll be damned," he finally said, sounding as shocked as she had been.

"You didn't know," she said.

"This is the first time I've heard anything about an adoption. I knew they'd wanted a child for years. Kevin worried about Grace after years went by without children. He said she'd always wanted a large family. Kevin eventually took her on an extended vacation to Europe, hoping to distract her from her sorrows. I didn't hear from them for several months until he showed up in my office one day, passing out cigars and beaming with the news that you'd been born. I remember teasing him that the vacation was obviously just what they had needed."

She could see the scene he'd described so clearly. Her breath hitched with her effort not to sob aloud.

"I need your help, George," she finally said.

"Name it."

"I want to hire someone to find my parents...my real parents."

"I'm not sure that's a good idea, Kelly," he immediately responded. "I know you're upset at the moment, but stop and think about this. There may be a very good reason why they kept your birth a secret. Are you sure you want to go digging around twenty-five-year-old secrets? There's no predicting what you might find."

"I'd rather know. Please understand. It's the not knowing. The thing is I don't know any investigators. I've never had reason to. Will you help me find one?"

"Well," he said, then paused. "If you're determined to do this, I do know of one man I would recommend without hesitation. He's one of the best."

"Who is he?"

"His name is Greg Dumas. He was a cop until some tragedy happened in his family that caused him to resign from the force. He opened an agency somewhere in Queens and has built a solid reputation for integrity. His agency has done work for my law firm on more than one occasion. I understand he's had to take on several associates to keep up with the work. Frankly, he'll probably be too busy to take the assignment himself, but if you can get him to do so, he'll be well worth his fee."

She took a deep breath and sighed with relief. She now had a name. She had a direction in which to go.

She wouldn't be sitting there wondering about her beginnings and unable to find answers.

"I'll call him," she said, feeling calmer already.

George gave her the investigator's office number and she hung up, staring at it. It was too late to call him this evening. She would call him first thing in the morning. Meanwhile…she had to get through the night.

When the phone rang near eight o'clock that evening, she felt she'd been given a reprieve from the questions revolving around in her head.

Her voice sounded hoarse from earlier crying. "H'lo."

"What's wrong?" Nick said immediately. "And don't play games with me. I can tell by your voice that something has upset you."

"I really can't talk about it right now," she said, tearing up again.

"I'll be right there," he said and hung up.

She stared at the phone in dismay. He was coming over now? But she didn't want to see anyone, especially Nick. She was feeling too vulnerable. And she really didn't know him well enough to share what she was going through with him.

Kelly called back but only got his terse voice mail. Resigned to the inevitable she went into the bathroom and washed her face, doing what she could to appear normal. Then she looked at herself in the mirror. Her eyes were red and swollen. Her nose glowed like a red neon sign. She looked awful and she just wanted to be left alone.

She had barely brushed her hair and washed her face with cool water when the doorbell rang. Bridget answered the door and Kelly heard Nick's low voice as she came down the stairs.

"I'm sorry, Mr. Chakaris, but Ms. MacLeod is not feeling well. I'll tell her that you stopped by—"

"It's okay, Bridget," Kelly said, walking toward them. "I was expecting him."

Nick looked at Kelly with concern. What had happened to cause her to be this upset? Nick wondered. He vaguely noted that Bridget had retreated toward the back of the house but at the moment he only had eyes for Kelly.

Without a word he walked over to her, wrapped her in his arms and held her closely against him.

He felt her stiffen and attempt to pull away but he didn't let go. He waited until she gradually relaxed against him. Only then did he lift her into his arms and carry her into the den.

He strode to one of the large leather chairs and sat down, holding her on his lap.

"Whatever's happened, I'll make it better, I promise. If someone has hurt you, I'll hunt him down and—"

She placed her fingers over his mouth. "It's nothing like that."

"So tell me."

She closed her eyes. "I uncovered some old family history I never knew about. It upset me, that's all. It has nothing to do with anything relevant to today. It was just the shock of discovery."

"I see." He waited and when she didn't say anything more, he asked, "Do you want to talk about it?"

She shook her head.

"I want to help you, Kelly. I have no ulterior motive."

"You can't, Nick," she said, straightening. She pulled away from him and stood. "I appreciate your stopping by, but really, there was no need."

He stood and stared at her. Her reluctance to share with him whatever had upset her stung him. He thought the past weekend had been a turning point in their relationship. She would never know how much restraint he'd exerted not to seduce her. Without vanity he knew he could have. Her response whenever he kissed her convinced him of the passion she kept so carefully hidden.

At the moment he wanted to smash his fist into a wall and howl. Instead, he nodded and walked out of the room. He arrived at the front door and was reaching for it when she spoke from somewhere behind him.

"Nick?"

He turned. "Yes?" A flicker of hope flared that she had changed her mind about talking to him.

"Thank you for coming by. I appreciate it. It's just that I have to deal with this on my own."

He could see she was still upset. Anything he might say would only upset her more. He nodded. "I'll call in a few days, if that's all right."

"Thank you." She followed him to the front door and let him out. He heard the bolt slide into place behind him and couldn't remember a time when he so wanted to be on the other side of a locked door.

He didn't like what was happening to him since he'd first met Kelly. Why was he insisting on forming a relationship with her? He'd never gone to this much trouble before over any woman.

She'd made it clear tonight that she was wary of him no matter what he did or said. Maybe it was time to cut his losses and forget about her.

Chapter Eight

Kelly arrived at the investigator's office promptly at two o'clock the next afternoon, the time he had set their appointment. She was grateful that he'd agreed to see her so promptly.

The woman seated behind a desk in the front office looked up and smiled when she saw Kelly.

"I'm Kelly MacLeod. I have an appointment with Mr. Dumas."

"I'll let him know you're here." After a brief dialogue on the phone the receptionist stood and said, "Please follow me." She walked along the hallway past two doors and opened the third. "Greg, this is Ms. MacLeod."

A tall, dark-haired man walked over to her and held out his hand. "I'm very pleased to meet you. George

Lancaster has referred several of his clients to me, which I appreciate. Please have a seat and I'll see what we can do to help you.''

Kelly studied the man while he walked behind the desk and sat down. He would make a wonderful brooding Darcy in the Jane Austen novel. He was almost as formidable looking as Nick had been the first day they'd met.

''What problem do you have that needs investigating?'' he asked.

She carefully folded her hands in her lap and said, ''I've just discovered that I was adopted. My parents are deceased, so I can't ask them to explain their secrecy. All I know is that my adoption papers came from Edinburgh, Scotland. I have the name of the solicitor and attending physician. I want to find my birth parents, Mr. Dumas. I'm willing to pay whatever's necessary for you to go to Scotland.''

He raised his brows. ''There are other ways to trace data, Ms. MacLeod, other than physically going there. The Internet has a considerable amount of information that we can go through and—''

She held up her hand and he stopped speaking.

''If that's all I needed—names and addresses—I could do that much myself. What I need, Mr. Dumas, is someone I trust to go there, meet with my birth parents and find out if they're willing to see me. I'd prefer to get your impression of them as well. As you can imagine, this has been quite a shock for me. I would imagine that a long-lost daughter suddenly turning up would be a shock to them as well.''

He studied her from beneath his brows. She didn't look away. Greg straightened and looked out the window.

When he looked back at her, he said, "I'm not sure that I'm the man to do the job for you, Ms. MacLeod. I've never taken an assignment that took me out of the country. Perhaps you should hire someone in Scotland to handle this assignment."

"I want someone I can trust, Mr. Dumas, and George trusts you implicitly. Therefore, I trust you." She straightened her shoulders and said, "If you will do this assignment for me, I'm willing to double your regular rate in addition to paying for all expenses."

He frowned. "I haven't told you what I charge."

"I'm aware of that. However, I doubt that you'd cheat me."

He finally smiled, which softened his face somewhat. "No, I won't cheat you." He nodded toward the envelope in her hand. "Is this the information you found?"

Kelly handed it to him. "Yes. Since there's no one on this side of the Atlantic left to question, I hope you can find someone over there."

"I can't guarantee that I'll be able to find what you're looking for."

She nodded. "I can live with that. Just do what you can."

He took the aged envelope and removed the documents inside. "I'll need a copy of these," he said. "I don't want to be responsible for the originals." When she nodded her agreement, he pushed a button on his desk. He waited a moment and said, "Sharon, I have documents that need to be photocopied."

"Yes, sir."

The receptionist was there within a minute or so. Less than five minutes later she returned with copies. Once Sharon left, Kelly said, "You appear to have a well-trained staff, Mr. Dumas."

"Yes, which is fortunate. Otherwise, I wouldn't consider an assignment that took me out of the U.S."

She liked the looks of the man and knew George wouldn't have suggested him if he had any doubts about the investigator's integrity. Kelly reached into her handbag and drew out a check. "I hope this will be enough to retain you," she said, handing it to him.

He glanced at the amount, then at her. "I hope I can live up to your expectations," he finally said. She admired the fact he didn't act coy about the large amount she was paying him.

She stood. "I'm going out of town for a while. I don't know how long I'll be gone. You won't need to keep me updated. If I'm still away when you return, just leave word with my housekeeper and I'll get back with you."

Greg walked around the desk when she stood and shook her hand once again. "I'll do the best I can," he said. "I hope to obtain the necessary information within a week, no more than two at the most." He walked her to the door. "I appreciate your confidence in me."

Kelly smiled. "Thank you for taking the case."

Only after she was in the taxi going home did Kelly

realize she was trembling. No matter how hard she tried, she couldn't get past the fact that her parents had gone to a great deal of trouble, as well as breaking who knows how many laws, to keep the adoption secret. Hadn't they trusted her to handle the news? Or was it something else?

She'd thought about going to Italy last week. Now she felt it was even more important to get out of the house she'd been raised in—a place that reminded her of her parents no matter which room she was in. She needed to put some distance between herself and Nick as well. She had come so close last night to pouring out all her grief, bewilderment and pain to him. She'd been afraid that if she attempted to discuss it with him she would have broken down and sobbed. Her humiliation would have been complete.

She'd contact her travel agent to find her a place to stay and to get her a ticket to leave as soon as possible.

As soon as she reached home, Kelly went down her list of current and prospective clients and phoned each of them. She explained that she would be away for a while. She would deliver the paintings she'd finished and put everything else on hold.

Most of them understood. Those who were incensed that she would postpone their sittings threatened to cancel. None of it mattered to her.

The following Monday afternoon Kelly boarded her flight to Rome. She'd made this trip several times and knew she would need to rest as much as possible on the plane. Because of the time change, tomorrow would be a long day.

She hadn't heard from Nick since the night he'd come over. Had that only been a week ago? So much had happened to her that his visit seemed to have been in another life, a fantasy from which she'd been abruptly awakened.

Now that she had time to think she wondered if she should have called to let him know her plans. Since he had not called her for a week—after calling her every day since they had met—Nick must have decided she wasn't worth pursuing. Kelly could only feel relief at the moment. She knew she wasn't thinking clearly and she didn't trust her feelings where he was concerned.

It was just as well for her to have this time alone to figure out what, if anything, she needed to do about Nick.

Her plane landed at Rome's Leonardo da Vinci airport at seven-thirty the following morning, even though her body insisted that it was the middle of the night. By the time she'd cleared customs and retrieved her rental car, it was ten o'clock local time.

She waited until she reached the outskirts of Rome before stopping to purchase bread, cheese and the largest possible container of coffee. According to the instructions she'd received, she had another three hours of driving before reaching the small villa she'd rented. It was located on the coast between San Vincenzo and Livorno.

Kelly had been told that a couple, Luis and Rosa,

would be there to look after her and the property, prepare meals, run errands and do anything else she might need. Their services were part of the rental price.

By the time she arrived, she felt like a zombie. She pulled into the circular driveway and stopped in front of the house, wondering if she had enough energy to get out of the car.

When a young man—Luis, no doubt—came bouncing down the wide, shallow steps to the car she almost hugged his neck out of relief. She wouldn't have to struggle with her luggage.

As soon as Kelly walked inside the house, she introduced herself to Rosa. When Rosa realized Kelly spoke fluent Italian, she burst into joyous laughter and speech.

Kelly explained that all she wanted to do was to go to bed and sleep around the clock. While she showered and changed out of her travel clothes, Rosa brought a light meal to the bedroom and poured some delicious-tasting wine.

Kelly didn't need wine to put her to sleep. By the time she slipped between the sheets she could scarcely keep her eyes open. Her last waking thought was to wonder what the rest of her new home was like.

When she woke early the next morning, Kelly felt much better. She slipped on her warmest robe and fleece-lined slippers and began to explore.

There was a living room with a wonderful view of the Mediterranean, two other smaller bedrooms, one of which she could use as a studio, and a charming kitchen.

She spotted several chairs and lounges arranged on the terrace near the French doors of the living room. Once curled up warmly, Kelly drowsed as dawn crept into the sky. Light clouds to the west caught the earliest rays of the sun and turned the sky into a palette of soft colors—a hint of pink, a touch of yellow—until the sun passed the horizon and burst into glorious color, returning the fleecy white clouds back to their natural hue.

The tranquility was exactly what she needed…that and the wonderful light that Italy produced. Her fingers itched to paint what she had seen. The house was on a slight elevation near the water and she could hear the soothing sound of the soft waves lapping against the shore.

"Good morning, Miss MacLeod," Rosa called out gaily in Italian.

Kelly glanced over her shoulder and smiled, the language melodious to her ears.

"May I bring you some coffee, perhaps, or some fruit? Or eggs?"

"Coffee and toast with some fruit sounds wonderful."

Rosa went into the house and Kelly stretched her arms high over her head. She felt decadent lazing around in her nightclothes with nothing planned for her day. Once dressed, she would start exploring the neighborhood. She'd never spent more than a weekend or so in Tuscany and was looking forward to visiting the villages and the countryside, sketching anything that caught her interest.

She was glad she had come.

* * *

A week later Nick sat at his desk, drumming his fingers. She hadn't called him. He'd given her some space—and himself as well—but he hadn't spoken to her in almost two weeks. Two weeks. He'd actually attended several social functions that, under normal circumstances, he would have skipped, in hopes of seeing her there. When he saw Comstock at one of them with another woman, he had conflicting feelings—he was disgruntled that he hadn't been successful in finding her and relieved that she wasn't with Will.

His emotions kept yo-yoing from one extreme to the other and he didn't like it.

He'd convinced himself to forget her and had been successful…for at least five minutes at a stretch during those two weeks. He'd picked up the phone to call her more times than he wanted to admit, even to himself.

Finally, he grabbed the phone and called, disgusted with his uncharacteristic wavering. It was a simple phone call, that was all. There was no harm in inquiring about her after leaving her in such distress.

He heard the phone being picked up and forced himself to breathe. He felt let down when he didn't hear Kelly's voice.

"MacLeod residence," Bridget said.

"This is Dominic Chakaris. I'd like to speak to Kelly, please."

"I'm sorry, but she's away for a while."

He stared at the receiver in disbelief. "Away?" he repeated. "As in out of town?"

"Yes, sir. She left for Italy last week and wasn't certain at that time when she might return."

"Thank you," he replied and slowly hung up the phone.

Italy, he mentally repeated. *Italy?* When had she planned a trip to Italy? He knew quite well that she had never once mentioned that she planned to be gone for an extended period of time. What was going on?

Nick glared at the phone, the unsuspecting messenger of this unsettling news. So. If there had ever been the slightest doubt in his mind, he now had his answer. She had no intention of developing a relationship with him. He recognized a lost cause when faced with one.

He would deal with how that knowledge made him feel later. Right now, he had a business to run...the very business that had convinced her he was slightly lower than a snake on the evolutionary scale.

Chapter Nine

Kelly sat before the fire curled up in a lap robe, reading. A rainstorm had sent her home early from her daily explorations. The rain continued to beat on the windows and doors, adding a rhythmic accompaniment to the snap and crackle of the fire.

During the three weeks since she'd arrived she had spent most of her days exploring and sketching and her evenings catching up on authors she enjoyed.

When she realized after the first week that she hadn't brought books, she'd gone onto the Internet and ordered them. Kelly had grown fond of the convenient way to shop and the quick response. Her order had arrived within the week.

She leaned her head against her chair and stared into the flames. She had needed this time away from everyone and everything. It had given her space to reflect on her life and to come to terms with the changes taking place.

During her solitary rambles she had deliberately recalled memories of her childhood and relived them. Her earliest memories were of laughing parents, applauding her every accomplishment, large or small.

Her seventh birthday stood out from the others. She'd had a party and invited all her school friends and her dad had stayed home to be a part of the celebration.

Her father had always been a major figure in her childhood. He was the one who read to her at night…not just the popular children's books of the day but stories by Robert Louis Stevenson and Charles Dickens. When she reached the age where she could appreciate the rhythm and phrasing of Shakespeare, he'd read the Bard's comedies to her. She'd fallen in love with the stories and characters and developed a keen appreciation for the written word.

During her stay in Tuscany, Kelly eventually came to terms with the knowledge that for whatever reason, her parents had chosen to give everyone the impression that she had been born to them. Knowing them as well as she did, she knew that they must have had a very good reason.

There were times when she thought about calling home to see if Greg Dumas had returned, but each time the thought had occurred she'd decided to wait. She needed time to prepare herself to hear whatever he had discovered. There would be time for her to listen and evaluate the information...but not now. Her idyllic days and peaceful nights were working their magic on her. There would be time enough to face her options regarding what to do next when she stepped back into her routine in New York.

Kelly had hoped that once she was in Italy she would no longer think about Nick. She'd been wrong. Whether she was relaxing or exploring, dreaming or awake, thoughts of him continued to pop into her head. A particularly lovely sunset one evening caused her to want to share the experience with someone...and that someone was always Nick, the man who had managed to disrupt her life.

There had been times when she wondered what he thought when he found she had left. Then she would remind herself that she hadn't heard from him at all during the week before she'd left. He probably didn't know she was gone.

By physically distancing herself from him, she'd given herself the space to look at his role in the family business more objectively.

She reviewed the facts. He'd seen a company in trouble. Knowing how much debt her father had left, despite the money he'd received from the sale of the company, caused her to question some of her assumptions about her father's role in the matter.

She recalled the struggle she and her mother had had to pay off debts by selling everything they owned—except for the house and furnishings—while Kelly supported them with her commissions.

Nick had made some valid points. Her father hadn't

been much of a businessman, she now realized. He'd been a wonderful husband and father and had no doubt done his best to keep the company going, but it hadn't been enough.

He'd been distraught, but was it because of his inability to save the company on his own or because someone else could? she wondered. Her father had never discussed business with her but his depressed state had cast a pall over the household until he died. Had worrying about the outstanding debt remaining been a more direct cause of his death?

How could she hold Nick responsible for that?

In an act of contrition, she decided to do another portrait of him. During the morning hours when the light was best in the room where she painted, she had sketched him as she remembered him in various moods. The tough negotiator would always be a part of who he was but during their weekend spent together she had discovered another man, a private man whom she'd found delightful.

He had a wicked sense of humor, an appreciation for Mother Nature's autumn palette, an ability to focus on whatever was going on around him. He aimed that same focus on her, listening intently when she shared something about herself with him.

That was the man she began to paint.

Now, as she stared into the flickering flames, Kelly thought about the painting that was almost done. This time she'd shown the humor in his eyes and his smile. She'd also portrayed him as quite a hunk. Allowing her imagination to run wantonly wild, Kelly had painted him reclining in bed, a sheet draped provocatively across his lower body.

What would have happened if she'd told him what had upset her the last time she saw him? He would have comforted her, she knew. Would that comfort have turned into something else? Would he have ended up staying with her that night? Would he have held her and made love to her and kissed away all her tears?

She shivered. Her imagination was a little too detailed for her peace of mind.

What should she do when she returned to New York? Call him, perhaps? Invite him over? Tell him she was ready to take their relationship to the next step?

Did she dare?

Some of her memories of the caustic way she had spoken to Nick during their meeting in his office made her flinch. She missed him. At least she could admit it to herself. However, she wasn't sure she could deal with her pain when their relationship ended, which it was sure to do once he grew tired of her.

She would be much better off keeping their relationship casual until he moved on.

"Where's that contract from San Francisco?" Nick asked tersely. "Have the new provisions been prepared by the legal department yet? And why did Wilson decide to back out of the limited partnership?"

Craig looked at Nick. Without a hint of his usual humor he said, "Maybe your charming disposition the last few weeks was too much for him and he decided the money he would make wasn't worth the aggravation.''

Nick's eyebrows lowered into a frown. ''What the hell is that supposed to mean?''

''It means that no one's been able to get along with you for weeks, that's what it means. What's the matter with you? I've seen you keep your cool when any other man would have completely lost control. Now you blow up over the most trivial things imaginable.''

''Neither the papers due from San Francisco nor the limited partnership is trivial,'' Nick snapped.

''Bawling out Evelyn because you ran out of staples is. Oh, and how about the tirade you launched yesterday because you couldn't find what you were looking for on your desk...which, by the way, is a disaster.''

Nick looked down. Craig was right. His normally neat desk had disappeared beneath papers strewn over the surface and stacks of files sliding into other stacks. The only neat thing about the desk was his stapler, refilled and carefully returned to the center.

He rubbed his eyes with the heels of his hands before shoving his fingers through his hair. When he finally met Craig's eyes, he gave him a half smile. ''That bad, is it?''

''Worse. I have a mutiny on my hands. I've been placed on notice that if I should ask any employee to come in here for any reason, that employee would immediately give notice.''

Nick blinked. ''Are you kidding me?''

Craig did not smile. ''No. In addition, I've put in

for combat pay for several of us who have to deal with you on a daily basis. Unfortunately I've been unable to explain your lousy mood to any of the staff or the number of potential clients and partners you've managed to piss off.''

Nick leaned his head against his chair and closed his eyes. He took several long, deep breaths and exhaled each time with a sigh. He had nothing to say to that. He sure as hell couldn't deny it. He owed everyone a rather large apology and he knew it.

He opened one eye. ''What do you think I should do to make amends?''

Craig pursed his lips. ''You might try sending flowers to everyone who's been the brunt of your unpredictable temper…and maybe attach a handwritten mea culpa to each one. That should keep you busy and out of mischief for a few days.''

''Damn.'' Nick straightened and glared at Craig. ''I am not sending you a bunch of flowers, much less a written note. Is this your idea of writing something on the board a hundred times?''

''Not quite that many, but at least you get the general idea. I'll do my best to live with the disappointment of not receiving flowers from you. The note doesn't matter. You wouldn't mean it anyway.''

When Craig closed the door behind him, Nick pushed his chair back and stood. He walked over to the window. He'd always enjoyed the view and felt he'd earned it by sheer dint of his will and determination. He'd spent years with a single-minded goal—

to make as much money as possible with dignity, honor and integrity.

He was a success. So why was he feeling that none of it mattered anymore? He'd been putting in eighty to eighty-five hours a week building his empire for years and had thought nothing of it. He'd built all of this from a vision he'd had as a teenager and he'd made it happen.

But he wondered if somewhere along the way he'd lost some of his humanity. Had he vented his irritation and frustration at his employees? Of course he had. Evelyn, especially, had been the unlucky person—besides Craig, of course—who'd been forced to put up with his moodiness.

Craig's remark about offending all the employees had been exaggerated. He hadn't seen most of his employees because he'd stayed hidden away in his office. A few department heads were the only people who had witnessed his short temper.

He shook his head in disgust at himself. He owed each of them a great deal. An apology wasn't a bad way to start.

He crossed the room and opened his door. Evelyn immediately looked up from her work and eyed him warily. "Evelyn," he said quietly, "Would you please come into my office?"

Since he normally used the intercom to summon her, her expression of wariness changed to dread. By the time he'd reseated himself at his desk she was seated across from him, pen and pad in hand.

He folded his hands and studied them for a moment

before raising his eyes and facing her. "I want to apologize for my behavior these past several weeks. It's been inexcusable. Now that Craig has brought it to my attention, I'm having some rather bad moments remembering how obnoxious I've been lately."

Evelyn, married and in her late thirties, smiled and said, "Apology accepted."

He raised a brow. "You shouldn't be so quick to absolve me, you know. I was willing to treat you and your husband to tickets to a Broadway show of your choice as well as any restaurant you fancied."

"Oh, you can do that, too. To salve your conscience."

He laughed. "You've got it. Name the day it would be convenient for you and I'll see—oh, wait. You're the one who arranges all of that for me. This time do it for yourself and put it on my personal account."

"Thanks."

He looked at his messy desk. "If I promise to use the manners my mother taught me, would you help me clear some of this stuff out of here before I'm engulfed and consumed by it?"

She chuckled. "I'd be delighted."

Kelly had walked farther today than she'd intended when she left home that morning and she knew her trek back to the villa would be an arduous one. She stopped in a small village and ate a little to keep her going until dinner.

She'd decided last night that she would return to New York in another week. As much as she enjoyed being here, she needed to get back to work...that is, if she had any commissions left when she returned.

She was pleased with the work she had done in Italy. A couple of the landscapes were among her best work. In the one of the villa, she'd caught the light at just the right angle, a difficult thing to do at the best of times. Now she would always have a reminder of this time of rejuvenation.

It was also time to face whatever information the investigator had found for her. He'd probably been back a few weeks, but at least she wouldn't have to wait for a report once she got there.

Her time away had done what she had needed... helped her to digest the recent events in her life and come to terms with most of them. She was ready to move on.

The sun hung just above the horizon by the time she trudged up the stairs to the villa. She'd passed the late model sports car parked in her driveway with a curious look. Maybe a friend of Luis's had stopped by. She was looking forward to throwing herself into a warm tub and soaking not only her tired feet but also the aches she'd acquired by overdoing it today.

She stepped inside and looked around the empty living room before going to the kitchen. Rosa stood at the stove stirring something delicious-smelling while she hummed a lilting tune.

"Hmm. That smells wonderful. By the way, whose car is that out front?"

Rosa turned and smiled at her. "You're later than

usual. You must be tired. The gentleman said he'd come from Rome and that you and he are friends.''

Perhaps it was someone she'd gotten to know when she'd went to school here. She had contacted a few since she'd first arrived. The timing wasn't all that great, though. Too bad he hadn't called first.

''Where is he now?''

''He said he would wait for you on the terrace and enjoy the view.''

Well, he could wait a little longer then, she decided, and went to her room where she rid herself of her clothes, showered and washed her hair. A friend would understand her need to clean up after a day of hiking.

When she combed the tangles from her wet hair she decided to leave it down to dry. She slipped into the warm lounging robe she liked to wear evenings, stuck her poor tired feet into soft slippers and went to greet her visitor.

She spotted him as soon as she stepped through the French doors onto the terrace. He stood with his back to her, his hands in his pockets, watching as the sun slid beneath the waves. At the moment she could only see his back.

She gaily called out in Italian, ''Welcome to my humble abode,'' and walked toward him.

When he turned toward her, he did not respond, but stood with his arms hanging at his sides, watching her approach.

Suddenly she could see his face.

It was Nick.

Kelly paused a few feet away and stared at him,

drinking in his features. As usual, he was dressed impeccably but his eyes looked tired and she noticed for the first time that he was graying slightly at the temples.

He didn't smile. He continued to stand there... watching her, waiting for her to say something now that she had recognized him.

The leap of joy her heart took when she realized who her visitor was told Kelly all she needed to know about her feelings for Nick.

Without a word she continued moving toward him until she was only a few inches away. Still without a word she slipped her arms around his neck and, clinging tightly, began to kiss him.

He stiffened at her touch and she suddenly realized—with acute embarrassment—that he hadn't come for the reason she'd first thought. She attempted to pull away but he wouldn't let her. Instead, he wrapped his arms around her in an oxygen-depriving grip and took over the kiss.

Chapter Ten

Nick knew he must be dreaming. He'd attempted to predict how Kelly might react to his showing up unannounced. As much as he had hoped, he hadn't expected her to be so welcoming.

He continued to kiss her until they both were gasping for air. He reluctantly slackened his hold on her and, as he expected, she stepped away from him. What he didn't expect was for her to say, "You once told me that we would not become intimate until I chose to do so." She took his hand and cradled it between hers. "Please make love to me, Nick," she whispered.

He couldn't believe what he was hearing. He'd never thought he'd hear Kelly utter those words. She led him inside her home and down a hallway. She paused in front of one of the open doorways.

With sudden impatience he picked her up and carried her over the threshold, shoving the door closed with his foot. He'd gotten an instant erection at her words and now trembled with his overwhelming need for her. He saw her bed and strode over to it. He placed her on the bed while he broke all records removing his clothes, pausing only long enough to remove protection from his wallet before lying beside her on the bed.

He pulled her close to his nude body, his hands moving restlessly over her. She wore some kind of flowing garment that felt so soft. He caressed the length of her spine, cupping her bottom and pulling her closer to him.

"We need to get you out of these clothes," he said, suiting his actions to his words.

She reached for the zipper that began at her throat and moved it downward. He assisted her until the garment fell open like wrapping paper revealing the gift inside.

Kelly was more beautiful than his imagination had managed to portray. Her high, delicately shaped breasts were covered with satin and lace. He ran his finger down between them and paused at her matching panties.

He fought to maintain some sort of control when all he could think about was kissing and caressing every inch of her body. He forced himself to slowly remove the lingerie and the robe until she was equally bare.

"I never thought I'd see you like this," he said, placing a kiss at her throat, another on the rosy tip of each breast. She inhaled sharply at his intimate touch. "I've wanted you forever, it seems," he added.

Shyly, she touched his bare shoulder and slid her hand across his chest, feeling the silky curls that quickly wrapped around her fingers.

"I don't want to rush you our first time together," he said, struggling for breath, "but I don't think I can wait much longer."

Her startled wide-eyed gaze provoked by his words made him want to laugh. He had to kiss her, no matter what happened. It was quite possible he'd embarrass himself if he weren't inside of her soon. The torment of wanting to love every inch of her before they joined battled with his rapidly slipping control.

Nick dipped his head to her breasts once more. She tasted so sweet. He wrapped his tongue around her hardened tip, pulling on it lightly until she gasped. He paused, afraid he'd hurt her until she arched her back, silently encouraging him. He stopped only long enough to don protection, before he lifted her mouth to his. He'd been starving for the taste of her. When she opened her mouth in silent surrender he teased her with his tongue, brushing her lips before exploring her mouth.

She boldly met his tongue, mimicking his moves until he slid his hand between her thighs. She gasped and nervously looked at him.

He cupped her and discovered she was damp and ready for him. Nick shifted until he was kneeling between her knees. Taking his time, he slowly eased inside her. And stopped, dismayed by how small she was. The last thing he wanted was to hurt her.

He started to withdraw when she wrapped her arms fiercely around his neck and her legs around his hips, locking her ankles. Nick shivered and lowered himself once again. This time she met him with a strong thrust of her hips, wresting control of their joining. He unintentionally went deep inside her until he was fully seated. The snug fit almost ended their lovemaking before it had begun.

He'd felt her flinch during that surge of joining and he held himself very still. "Did I hurt you?" he asked.

"I, uh, didn't know you were so big," she managed to say, panting.

He rested on his forearms to protect her from his weight. At her words, he leaned down and gave her a quick kiss, his tongue circling her lips. "And I didn't expect to find you so—so—" he searched for a word to express how small she was.

"So inexperienced?"

That's when it dawned on him. This was her first time with a man. The knowledge should have dampened his ardor but he couldn't help the sense of possession that swept over him at the thought that he was the first man to make love to her.

If he had his way, he would also be her last.

He began to withdraw slightly and she clung tightly to him.

"That wasn't what I was thinking at all," he said, placing tiny kisses along her temple and jaw. "I don't want to hurt you, that's all."

"The only way you can hurt me is to stop."

Nick knew he could never be that chivalrous. His noble intentions forgotten, he started rocking against her in a slow, easy movement, allowing her time to adjust to him.

He wanted to make this a good experience for her. He was rewarded when she came apart in his arms with a cry of surprise. He could feel her body convulsing around him, squeezing him until he could no longer resist giving in to his own need. With one last surge he climaxed with such intensity it was almost painful. He pressed his forehead into the pillow beside her head and fought for breath. After a few deep lung-filling breaths he rolled to his side, his arms wrapped firmly around her.

When he had the energy to move, he released her and went into the adjoining bathroom. When he returned, Kelly was propped up against pillows, the covers pulled to her shoulders, looking for all the world like a kid at Christmas finally discovering what Santa had brought.

Whatever else had happened while she was away, he was relieved that she was no longer looking at him with anger or resentment.

He lifted the sheet and used the damp washcloth to remove the evidence of her loss of virginity. When he returned to bed the second time he slipped beneath the covers and pulled her to his shoulder. "You don't need to be quite so modest, you know. Not after what we just did."

She buried her head in his shoulder. "I'm not used to someone bathing me," she muttered.

"I know this was painful for you and I'm sorry. The last thing I wanted to do was to hurt you."

"It only hurt at the beginning. I had no idea…"

"About what?"

"That lovemaking could feel so…so…I don't know the words to use."

He brushed his hand down along her side, trailed his fingers back up her spine, and felt her shiver. He turned and placed her on her back. He took his time exploring her with his mouth and hands, until she was begging him for relief.

He slipped his hand between her legs and gave her the release she needed. When she came apart he held her in his arms until she relaxed against him.

Pleasuring her without thought to his own desires was something new for him. He'd never before been so conscious of his partner's needs and wants and desires. He tried to figure out what that meant about him but at the moment was too relaxed to do more than give it a fleeting thought.

Content to lie there holding her, Nick thought Kelly had fallen asleep when she stirred.

"I was so tired when I arrived home this evening that all I wanted was a soaking bath and bed. I'm amazed that I completely forgot about all of that when I saw you standing there on the terrace."

"You surprised me, you know. I was half expecting you to banish me from your home. My highest hope was that you would talk to me." He kissed her bare shoulder. He was content to lie there and enjoy the comfortable silence that had fallen.

"How did you find me?" she finally asked, her fingers brushing the fine hair on his chest.

"Was it supposed to be a secret?"

"Not really. I was just surprised to see you, that's all."

"If your greeting was any sign of how you react to being surprised, be assured I'll do my best to surprise you on a regular basis."

She tugged on the chest hair between her fingers. "I'm being serious, here."

"Ouch." He lifted her fingers and kissed each tip. "Me, too. I can't remember when I've been this serious about anything." He smiled. "I hate to guess how long it's going to be before I'll want to let you out of this bed."

"Oh." She looked at him in surprise. "I thought that most men, once they'd made love to a woman, were no longer interested in her."

"Ah, so you're back with the insults, are you? I don't consider what other men do as having anything to do with me."

She moved so that she faced him. "I didn't mean to offend you. It's just that all this is new to me and I'm not sure what the etiquette is."

"Neither am I. Why don't we forget about rules and be honest with each other."

"I thought we were."

"More honest, then. For example, why did you leave New York without telling me?"

He sounded hurt, which surprised her. She thought he might be irritated...maybe angry, but not hurt.

"I'm not certain I can give you a rational explanation. At the time I left, I felt overwhelmed by so many things that were happening to me...I was suffering from a sort of sensory overload, I suppose. I needed to get away, go into some sort of retreat mode, and look at my life from a new direction."

"I thought you were running away from me."

She nodded. "Maybe I was...partially. I hadn't expected to discover so many different facets to your personality as I did during our weekend in New England. I'll admit I was shaken by them as well as being more than a little ashamed for the portrait I'd painted of you."

"Mmm. It's tough when facts screw up our preconceptions, isn't it?"

She nodded slowly. "I was still angry about who you were in relation to my family...and yet...getting to know you forced me to look at my father in a different way. He was always such a wonderful father and I'll admit I idolized him. I didn't want to see that he might have any imperfections."

He pulled her closer and kissed her temple. "Then please, whatever you do, don't ever idolize me, because I am full of imperfections."

She made no effort to hide her amusement. "Oh, I don't think we have to worry about that happening."

"Low blow, low blow. My ego doesn't stand a chance around you, does it?"

"Poor dear," she replied, kissing him on his cheek.

After a lengthy pause, she said, "Being alone here gave me time to think about a lot of things, including my confused and contradictory feelings for you. I had to sort through a lot of things. I suppose…and you wanted honesty here…in a way I *was* running away from you."

He stiffened and she kissed his jaw, running her hand along his chest down to his abdomen. He cleared his throat before asking, "Do you still want to run from me?"

She trailed her fingers down his body until she brushed against his rapidly hardening erection. "Do I look like I'm running?"

Before she knew it, he had flipped her onto her back, quickly grabbed another foil package to cover himself, and slid into her.

The feeling was indescribably delicious, and she made a small sound of pleasure.

He stopped. "I'm sorry. You must be sore. I don't know what I was thinking. I—"

"—think too much, as I've pointed out before. Don't start something you don't intend to finish, Mr. Chakaris."

"Whatever you say, Ms. MacLeod. Your wish is my pleasure to obey."

Kelly slowly came awake the following morning, wondering why she ached so. Her entire body protested when she started to stretch. Of course she'd overdone her hiking yesterday. Plus—

She jerked up into a sitting position and looked beside her.

Nick lay on his stomach, sound asleep, his head halfway beneath his pillow.

So she hadn't dreamed his appearance in Italy, after all. Kelly had a strong urge to stroke his back, since all of it was in view. The sheet lay just below his waist, displaying his strong, healthy body. He was magnificent-looking; there was no other word to describe him.

She gazed at what she could see of his face, more relaxed than she'd ever seen him. His profile could be found on many Greek statuaries. She envied him the long, black eyelashes that framed his oh-so-expressive eyes. She could already think of some changes she wanted to make to her latest painting of him. She'd get rid of the modestly draped sheet, for one thing. Now that she had actually seen him in all his glory, she had no intention of denying herself the opportunity of looking at him to her heart's content.

They hadn't talked much last night. He hadn't told her why he had come or how long he intended to stay. She decided not to question her good fortune. Instead, she would accept what he was willing to give and demand nothing more.

Chapter Eleven

Nick slowly surfaced from a deep sleep. He felt so relaxed he wasn't certain he could move if he tried. Not that it mattered. He had no desire to stir at the moment.

He lay there drifting in and out of sleep when the events of the previous night drifted into his consciousness. Suddenly awake, he opened his eyes and looked at the other side of the bed. There was no sign of Kelly. He glanced at his watch and saw that it was almost noon.

He'd never slept so long in his life. What was the matter with him? He started to get up and remembered that his suitcase was still—he stopped when he saw his bag sitting on a nearby table.

Nick relaxed a little and looked around. He hadn't

paid attention to anything except finding the bed the night before. The room was large and filled with sunlight. The furniture looked custom made, considering the way each piece had its own particular niche.

After he retrieved fresh clothes and his shaving kit, Nick took a long shower and thought about the night before.

Kelly had caught him off guard when she first appeared yesterday. Not that he was complaining. This was the relationship he'd hoped for. Her wholehearted response to his lovemaking confirmed his earlier conjecture…her cool and classic persona hid a woman of stunning sensuousness.

While he dried off, Nick wondered about her mood this morning. Her explanation for not letting him know when she left New York rang true. As long as they were honest with each other, their relationship had a chance of working for both of them.

They would talk more about their situation today, although the idea of keeping her in bed while he was there appealed to him even more.

He shaved, dressed in casual clothes and went in search of Kelly. He found her on the terrace, sketching. She glanced up when he stepped outside and gave him a friendly smile. "Good morning. I'll have Rosa bring you some coffee and something to eat. I imagine you could use some nourishment by now."

Her impersonal friendliness threw him. He hadn't given any thought to what he expected of her this morning, but her greeting was one she might give an aunt, not her lover. She gave no sign that she had any memory of being in bed with him last night.

He'd have to see how this morning played out. Adopting her casual attitude, he walked to the table where she sat, shaded by an umbrella, and took the other chair. "Coffee sounds good. I'll need to become more awake before I try much else."

Kelly went in search of Rosa and Nick gazed out over the peaceful view of land and water. When he'd first arrived he had thought that this was the perfect place to enjoy a sunset. Now he realized that the area was just as spectacular in the middle of the day.

When Kelly returned with a small tray holding a large carafe and cups, he stood and took them from her. "I told her to bring you something to nibble on, some fruit as well as her melt-in-your-mouth coffee cake."

He waited until she was in her chair before saying, "I apologize for sleeping so late."

"No apology necessary," she replied airily. "Your body's clock is telling you that it's around six o'clock in the morning. I guessed that you might be surfacing soon."

He sat in silence through his first cup of coffee and most of the second, adjusting to this new Kelly. Her bright voice and trembling hand signaled to him that she wasn't quite as casual and carefree as she wanted him to think. She'd adopted her social voice, which he'd never heard before…at least from Kelly.

Rather than question her, he decided to wait and see what she might do or say next.

Kelly looked relieved when Rosa brought a platter of delicacies to choose from together with service for two. She made all the appropriate sounds of appreciation. Once Rosa returned inside, Nick said mildly, ''I hope you didn't wait for me to join you before you ate.''

''Oh, no, not at all. This is my second meal of the day. Give your body time to adjust. By the way, how is it you happen to be in Tuscany? You were the last person I expected when I saw your car in the driveway.''

Nick had spent the flight across the Atlantic trying to come up with a plausible reason for finding her that wouldn't make her run even farther away. He decided on a half truth or two.

''There were a couple of business associates in Rome who've been asking me to visit in order to discuss a possible acquisition. Plus, my brother called to say he would be working in this general area for several weeks and suggested I fly over here to meet him.''

''When did you arrive in Rome?''

''About three days ago. I left word with my brother's agency to alert him that I'm here. He'll call my cell phone sometime in the next few days.'' He yawned and hastily covered his mouth. With a rueful smile, he said, ''I thought I'd adjusted to the time change. Obviously I haven't.''

''How long do you intend to stay?'' she asked, as though his answer had nothing to do with her.

He filled his cup once again and took a sip before answering. ''That depends on you.''

She blinked. He could feel her retreating from him even though she hadn't moved. "Me?" she asked, raising a brow. "How so?"

"I'd like to spend some time with you if you're willing to have me. If not, I'll return to Rome this afternoon and get out of your hair." She'd been watching him intently since she'd rejoined him. Had he spilled something on his clothes? He touched his open collar. "Is something wrong?"

She smiled. "I've never seen you looking so relaxed. I find the change interesting."

Nick self-consciously ran his hand through his hair. "I realized that I needed to take some time off. The trip has been good for me."

She leaned her elbows on the glass table and rested her chin on her clasped hands. "As far as your visiting me, I have no problem with you being here. There are two other bedrooms if you prefer to sleep alone."

Which wasn't exactly what he'd hoped she would say...especially after last night. In fact, she was continuing to act as though last night hadn't happened, as though losing her virginity was no big deal.

Well, it sure as hell was a big deal to him. "Do you mind if we discuss last night?" he finally asked.

A faint blush filled her cheeks, although her gaze didn't waver. "I'm not certain what there is to discuss. We're both single. We're young, healthy and enjoy each other in bed. What more is there to discuss?"

He eyed her with suspicion. Where had she gotten that particular speech, he wondered. It was close to the one he gave to a woman at the beginning of a relationship. He made sure the woman understood that there were no ties being forged, no commitment on either side and each of them was free to end the relationship at any time.

Nick had never given much thought to how it felt to be on the receiving end of such an announcement. He was discovering that it was painful…at least for him…because he wanted so much more with Kelly. Not that he'd given much thought to how much more…until now. Hearing her casually toss his philosophy back at him was a little unnerving.

He cleared his throat. "All right. As long as we both understand the rules," he replied.

"Oh, I've always understood the rules where you're concerned. Originally I had no intention of getting involved with you. However, the last few weeks have given me a chance to look at my life. I decided it was time for me to spread my wings, make new memories—" she waved her hand, encompassing their surroundings. "And your showing up was an opportunity for me to discover more about myself."

Nick wasn't sure why he felt disgruntled. Maybe it was because she'd reduced what they shared last night to one more step in her journey of self-discovery. "I'm glad I could be of service," he muttered.

She laughed. "I couldn't have chosen anyone better suited for an affair." She rose and held out her hand. "C'mon. The water in the pool should have warmed up enough by now. Let's change into swimsuits and enjoy the pool."

He stood and took her hand and they walked back to her room.

Nick noticed that Rosa had been in to make the bed, and his suitcase lay open on the table. ''Once you decide where you want to sleep, Rosa will unpack for you.''

He'd never spent an entire night with anyone before. He'd never liked having to face a woman the next morning and make casual conversation. Maybe that's why he was so bad at it.

As though he weren't there, Kelly opened a drawer and pulled out a couple of bright red strings. With economical movements she stripped out of her clothes and tied the strings around her body.

He did a double take. She wasn't going to wear that thing out of the room, was she? The thong bottom barely covered her mound. The rest of her was bare. Once she tied the strings at the top—behind her neck and chest—he wondered why she bothered wearing anything at all.

He forced himself to turn away and riffled through his clothes. Damn, he was already as hard as a rock. Which was crazy. After last night, he would have expected to stay dormant for a while.

Not to be outdone by her show of nonchalance, he removed his clothing and stepped into his swim trunks.

Kelly returned from the bathroom with towels and sunscreen and they returned outside without speaking.

He wished he knew what she was thinking…and feeling. There was no hint of the woman he'd met—

how long was it?—several weeks ago. He watched her go to the side of the pool and dive in. Her so-called suit wouldn't be able to withstand that kind of treatment without falling apart.

He grinned. Come to think of it, he had no reason to complain—as long as he was the only one to see her.

He might as well kick back and take advantage of some time away from the business world. The situation was perfect for him—a beautiful, intelligent woman; a utopian-type setting; hired help to take care of everything. He would be a fool not to enjoy every minute of it.

Once in the pool Nick swam leisurely laps until he grew bored. He swam closer to Kelly, ducked under the water and came up between her legs, her thighs around his neck. He heard her startled squeal when he came up for air and tipped her backward into the pool.

She came up sputtering, trying not to laugh. "Oh, it's war you want, is it?" she said, and made a dive for him. She swam underwater like a fish, darting here and there, as elusive as an eel.

By the time they paused for breath they were both laughing and Nick couldn't remember ever feeling quite this young.

Her face glistened with sparkling drops of water and her pale hair fanned out around her shoulders like a shawl. Nick grabbed her and kissed her before she had a chance to elude him once again.

Instead of fighting him, she wrapped her arms around his neck, her legs around his waist, enthusiastically returning his kiss. She tasted delicious and he couldn't get enough of her. He dipped his head so that he was partly submerged and could reach her nipples. He nudged the small covering aside, grateful she wore so little, and suckled her until he was forced to come up for air.

She gave a soft moan when he released her and moved her hips into him. He could feel her against his rock-hard erection as she continued her invitation…an invitation he had no intention of refusing. It was easy enough to shift the small triangle and smoothly enter her, their bodies plastered together.

"Ohhh," she murmured. "That feels so goo-ood." The hitch in her breath came when he almost withdrew before surging into her again. She felt weightless in his arms. He moved faster and faster until she came apart in his arms. Despite everything he could do to stop, he exploded deep inside of her, his body determined to mate with hers without anything between them.

Some part of Nick's mind reminded him that he never had sex without protection but at the moment, he didn't care. Instead, he stayed inside of her, holding her close and caressing her back as she lay limply against him.

Eventually she lifted her head and stared into his eyes, her blue ones sparkling. "Wow."

He grinned. "I'll second that." He looked around the pool. "I don't know about you but I think I'm ready for a nap. Care to join me?"

Her eyes rounded in surprise. "Oh. Well, I suppose so."

He reluctantly moved away from her and adjusted his suit, then took great pleasure in doing the same for her.

Once out of the pool, they shivered in the cool air and wrapped themselves with the bath towels before going inside. Nick escorted her to her room and closed the door behind them. He went over to the three wide windows and pulled the wooden shutters closed, adjusting the slats until there was a dim light in the room.

Nick turned and saw that Kelly had gone into the bathroom. He followed her, turned on the shower and led her inside. In a couple of movements, they were both bare. He took his time soaping her body, turning her from one side to the other to rinse off.

Kelly took the soap from him and did the same for him. As soon as she touched him, he was once again engorged. He shook his head slightly in amusement and amazement at the effect even a simple touch from her had on him.

After drying both of them, he walked back into the bedroom and pulled the sheets back, neatly folding them at the bottom of the bed. He glanced over his shoulder and caught Kelly eyeing his back. She still held her towel around her. He turned and plucked it from her, falling on the bed with his arms around her.

"You're really that sleepy?" she asked, "that you need another nap?"

"Oh, did I say nap? Hmm. Well, no, I'm not at all

sleepy. Maybe we can think of something else to do as long as we're here.''

He moved between her legs and leaned over her, placing what he'd intended to be a soft kiss on her mouth. Her response caused him to deepen the kiss and he became distracted from his original intentions.

During the kiss she reached for him and he gently pushed her hand away. When he paused for breath, he said, "This is for you, okay?"

"What do you mean?"

He set out to show her.

Nick took his time as he trailed kisses along and over her body. By the time he reached the thatch of hair at her thighs, she was squirming. "What are you—? No, please, I—ooohhh—" she whimpered. He continued to stroke her with his tongue, sliding his hands beneath her bottom and lifting her to his mouth.

When she climaxed he shifted so that he lay beside her. He held her as she draped herself limply across him.

"That wasn't fair. You didn't get to…"

"My pleasure comes in seeing the look on your face when you shatter into a climax. There will be other times. Just relax and enjoy."

Nick closed his eyes again and a few minutes later Kelly saw that he was asleep.

She lay there and looked at him. He looked so peaceful lying there. He'd been driving himself at such a hard pace for so long that once he stopped to relax, his body insisted on catching up. Kelly knew from experience that he would feel almost drugged for the next few days, much as she had, until he caught up on his rest.

Kelly slipped into the bathroom and showered. She wasn't sleepy at all. She was too caught up in all the new sensations she'd experienced in the past eighteen hours. She couldn't believe they had actually made love in the pool.

Her heart began to race. The pool. Here she'd been doing her best to act sophisticated and knowledgeable about these things and she never once thought of protection. She mentally calculated where she was in the month but soon gave up. She'd never been regular. She had no idea if she was safe from pregnancy or not.

She touched her abdomen. As much as she would love to have Nick's baby, she knew there was no way he would accept such a thing. If she was too naive to use protection, she knew it would be up to her to deal with the consequences.

After a quick shower, she dressed and went in search of something substantial to eat. Talk about building up a raging appetite. She couldn't remember another time in her life when she'd eaten so voraciously.

No one was in the kitchen when she walked in. She made herself a couple of sandwiches, poured iced tea and sat at the small table in the bay window.

Well, she had done it. She was having a flaming affair with the man she'd intended to hate forever. She seemed to have left that young woman behind somewhere, the one who saw everything in black and white.

Perhaps it was discovering the mystery of her birth or being exposed to a man who made her body quiver like a tuning fork whenever he walked into the room. Whatever happened, she was determined to treat his visit as a dream lifted out of time and space. She would enjoy every moment, refuse to discuss any serious subject with him and return home as though nothing out of the ordinary had happened.

All she had to do was continue to hide from Nick the fact she'd hidden from herself these past weeks—she had fallen in love with him, despite her original feelings toward him. She loved that he didn't apologize for who and what he was. She loved his take-me-or-leave-me attitude. She wasn't foolish enough to think she would ever have something permanent with him.

What she had now was enough. It would have to be.

Kelly rolled over early one morning to cuddle against Nick and discovered he wasn't in bed. She opened her eyes and looked around the empty room. How strange. For the past ten days, he'd awakened her each morning stroking her into arousal.

Not a bad way to start the morning, she thought, stretching. Last night they'd discussed her plans to return to New York. She'd postponed leaving for a week once he arrived. Instead she'd booked a flight for the following week. He'd driven to Rome several times on business, but was always home by the time she went to bed.

When he had remained at the villa, she'd taken him to some of her favorite places in Tuscany. He looked younger now than when he'd arrived...the strain in his face had disappeared. Oh. And his laugh. She adored his laugh. It was so wholehearted and infectious. She should have known from the first day they met what a tease he was.

She tried to remember if today was one of the days he was going to Rome but couldn't recall his mentioning it. He never discussed his business dealings, which was fine with her. The person she had been who had contemplated stopping him at all costs had morphed into a person who believed in him and his integrity.

In other words, she had grown up, no longer blaming him for everything that had happened in her life. She missed both of her parents but had finally come to terms with their passing.

Kelly showered and dressed, tying her hair into a bouncy ponytail. Nick enjoyed touching her hair—if his habit of frequently running his fingers through it was any indication. After the fourth time he'd pulled it out of the twist that was her usual way of dealing with it, she'd given up, wearing it down most of the time. But sometimes she liked to get it off her neck.

She headed toward the kitchen and paused when she heard the murmur of deep voices on the terrace. Did Rosa have repairmen here for some reason she hadn't mentioned?

When she looked outside, she saw that Nick hadn't

left. He was listening to a man who had his back to Kelly. She stepped outside, catching Nick's attention.

He immediately stood, holding his hand out to her and said, "Here she is now. You can see for yourself."

The other man stood and turned. He was a couple of inches taller than Nick but other than that, they looked very much alike. This must be his brother, Luke. When she drew closer she could see more subtle differences between them. Even if she hadn't already known that Luke was older, his craggy face and somber eyes gave him away. Luke's black eyes looked as though he'd visited hell on more than one occasion...and expected to go back.

When she reached the men, Nick pulled her against his side and said, "Kelly, this is my brother, Loukus Chakaris. I'd about given up on his being able to visit me this trip. Then he called early this morning and showed up about dawn." He grinned at his brother. "This is Kelly MacLeod, Luke, our gracious hostess."

Before letting go of her, Nick turned her toward him and kissed her lightly on the mouth. "Good morning, Ms. MacLeod. You're looking quite rested this morning. I hope you slept well."

Kelly knew she was blushing but there was no help for it. He knew quite well how much—or rather how little—sleep she'd managed to get the night before. He chuckled at her embarrassment.

"Here, sit down. There's coffee and some of Rosa's famous rolls and muffins for you."

He pulled out a chair and once she was seated, he and Luke followed suit.

"I'm so glad you were able to come visit Nick," she said with pleasure. "Nick speaks very highly of you and I've been looking forward to our meeting."

"Then you have the advantage," Luke replied in a deep and rumbling voice. "I've only learned about you since I arrived this morning. Nick said he was staying with someone. He didn't say who."

Nick poured Kelly some coffee and moved the basket of hot breads closer. "I wanted to surprise you," he replied. "This is the first time I've taken off in more years than I can recall." He gave Kelly a wicked side glance. "It's been very relaxing for me."

The way he said the word implied anything but. She refused to comment on his teasing. She helped herself to some rolls and fruit and listened while the men continued their conversation.

Luke doesn't smile much, she thought, then realized with something of a shock that Nick had never smiled when she first met him. What a change in him since he'd arrived here.

She listened with amusement while he told Luke about the places they'd explored and how serene he'd found her villa.

Luke made all the right replies and told them about several places he'd visited in Italy when he'd had an opportunity.

The conversation was light and impersonal. *We could be filming a travelogue for all the depth of our conversation.*

When Kelly finished her meal and was enjoying another cup of coffee, Nick stood and said, "I hate to leave pleasant company but Craig set up a conference call later this morning and I need to be ready." He brushed his knuckles over her cheek. "I'll leave the two of you to visit and get better acquainted."

Kelly watched with dismay as Nick disappeared into the house. He knew his brother better than she did, but from his expression and body language it seemed to Kelly that Luke would have much preferred to spend his time with Nick.

Not that she blamed him. She gave him a rueful smile. "That's Nick for you. Always busy, always working on the next venture." She held up the carafe and asked, "Would you care for more coffee?"

"Please," he said quietly, edging his cup closer to her. "Nick tells me you're an artist."

"Yes."

"Is it a hobby or a profession for you?"

"Both, probably. I guess I haven't thought about it from that perspective."

"He said you painted a rather startling likeness of him. I'd like to see it sometime."

Kelly had a sudden vision of the painting hidden in the room she was using as a studio...the nude painting she worked on whenever Nick was away.

"It's in New York. Do you visit there much?"

"Not if I can help it. I prefer Europe."

"Oh." For the life of her, Kelly couldn't think of another topic to discuss. The only thing they appeared to have in common was their connection to Nick and her connection was tenuous at best.

Luke broke the silence between them after several minutes and asked, "How long have you known Nick?"

"We met a few months ago, although I've known who he was for several years. I feel as though I've known him forever."

"How did you meet?"

She smiled. "Through the painting you mentioned. I painted his portrait and it was shown with the rest of my work at an art gallery."

He raised an eyebrow, reminding her of how much he looked like Nick. "I'm not following you. You met him and painted his portrait? Did he commission it?"

"We hadn't actually met until after the painting was shown."

"Interesting. And your reason for choosing him to paint was—what, exactly?"

"It probably won't make much sense, but I was going through a tough time and his face kept appearing in my head. I finally put it on canvas so he would stop haunting me."

"Haunting you," he repeated.

She cleared her throat. "It seemed like a good idea at the time. He contacted me after it had been put on display and asked me to lunch. I accepted and we've been in touch since then."

He studied her without expression for a moment or two, then said, "I suppose it was one way to meet the man who you say haunted you."

She felt more uncomfortable with each question and comment Luke made. Perhaps this was just his style, but she felt like she was being interrogated.

"Well, I suppose that's one way of looking at it. It certainly wasn't a conscious decision I made at the time, though."

"Nick said you've been here for several weeks. What prompted you to come to Italy?"

That was an easier question to answer and she felt the tension leaving her shoulders. "I spent a year in Italy while I was getting my education. I felt the need to get away from New York for a while and decided to come here. Nick found me here ten days ago."

"I see," he said thoughtfully and she wondered what exactly he thought he was seeing.

Did he think she was playing hard to get so that Nick would follow her here? If so, he couldn't be more wrong. Part of the reason she'd left was to get away from him and clear her mind. However, she felt no need to justify her behavior to Luke.

Kelly gazed off toward the calming view, striving to relax and hoping that Nick would return soon. When she turned her gaze back to Luke, she realized he was watching her intently.

"Nick tells me you work for the government in some kind of hush-hush capacity."

Luke's mouth quirked into a slight smile. "That's as good an explanation as any, I suppose."

"You must enjoy your work."

His smile disappeared and he was silent for a moment, as though remembering something. "It's trite to say that someone has to do it, but in my case, that's the way I feel.''

Whatever he'd recalled brought back the somber look.

''When was the last time you were home?''

''It's been a while.''

''Oh. Nick mentioned that his parents were gone. Was that recent?''

He'd been lighting a cigarette when she spoke and paused abruptly at her question. After staring at her for a moment, he finished lighting his cigarette and inhaled deeply before he replied. With yet another question.

''What has Nick told you about our family?'' he asked, crossing his arms and leaning them on the table.

Surprised by the question, Kelly replied, ''Very little. He mentioned once that he was raised in the Bronx and that you're his only living relative. Why?''

''Because knowing where we came from might better explain the man you're involved with.''

''Oh.''

''Our parents were immigrants, hoping to find a better place to bring up a family. They moved into a tenement in the Bronx, the only place they could afford even though it was a rough neighborhood. They never said anything but I'm sure it didn't help matters when I was born. They always said that money didn't really matter...they had what they'd always wanted. Family.

''Dad found a job working in a factory where the hours were long and the pay ridiculously low, even for the times. To supplement their income, Mother cleaned houses. They arranged their schedules so that one of them was always with me.'' He sounded hoarse and picked up a water glass in front of him, draining it. ''Nick was born when I was two. Our sister came a year later.''

Kelly blinked in surprise. ''Your sister?''

''She died before she was two because my parents had no insurance and when she contracted pneumonia her second winter, they couldn't afford the hospital charges and didn't know where to go for help. They tried remedies from the Old World but nothing helped and she died in Mother's arms.''

''Oh, my God,'' Kelly whispered, pressing her fingers to her mouth.

His voice remained level as he continued. ''Our second sister was born when I was ten. Nick and I were both working after school by that time…helping out at the neighborhood grocery, running errands. You name it, we did it.''

With an almost violent shove away from the table, Luke stood and walked to the low wall at the edge of the terrace. He rubbed the back of his neck and stared at the water as though to give himself some time.

Several minutes of silence passed before he turned to face her. ''Elena was six when she was killed by a stray bullet because she happened to be playing with a friend on our front stoop when gang members decided to destroy a few members of a rival gang.''

Suppressed anger rolled off him in almost visible waves. ''I quit school right after that and got a full-time job to try and make enough money to get them out of there. I bullied Nick into staying in school. Despite his reluctance, he stayed and continued to work evenings and weekends.''

''I had no idea,'' she whispered, appalled by what the Chakaris family had gone through.

''Dad got sick that winter. He had changed jobs and he was supposed to be covered by the insurance furnished by his new employer, but the company found some nit-picking reason to deny the claim. The illness was too much for his heart. He'd worked too many years pulling down long hours and double shifts. He'd literally worked himself to death. He'd just turned fifty.

''Our mother died a few months later. Both of our parents worked themselves into an early grave, trying to provide for us. The doctor found a label to put on their death certificates—natural causes—but Nick and I knew better. Poverty killed them.

''When Elena was killed, Nick swore that he was going to do whatever it took to make as much money as he could. He was going to take care of our parents, build them a mansion to live in…he was going to be a millionaire by the time he was thirty.'' A half smile formed on his lips. ''Damned if he didn't meet his goal. But it didn't seem to matter much to him by then. Our parents have been gone a long time.

''Nick was determined to go after the factory owners who paid slave wages and few benefits. They were the same kind of people who hired Mother to clean their houses for less than a minimum wage. He has no use for the rich who live off the poor.

"Isn't it ironic that he now moves in the same circles as they do? Not only that, but he's having an affair with one of them."

Kelly swallowed, her mind reeling with this new insight into Nick. "My father," she said slowly, "owned one of the businesses taken over by Nick's corporation. But he wasn't like that. He paid good wages with strong benefits."

"I see. So he allowed Nick to buy his holdings. Interesting."

She looked down at her hands, which were gripped tightly in her lap. "He was too heavily mortgaged to stop Nick from taking over."

"Really. And yet you actively pursued the opportunity of meeting him by displaying your portrait of him for all to see."

"I didn't paint it in order to meet him."

"Didn't you? Well, only you know your motives, of course. It seems to me you've created the opportunity to take Nick for a ride as some sort of payback." Once again he stood. "Just so we're clear on this, if you end up hurting my brother, Ms. MacLeod, you can rest assured you'll answer to me." Luke turned and walked into the house.

Kelly was so shaken she could hardly move from her chair. As soon as she could manage, she went inside. She paused, listening for the sound of a voice, but she could hear nothing...not even Nick on the phone.

She went to her room and found Rosa gathering up the linens she'd just taken off the bed. Kelly nodded to her and sat on the side of the newly made bed. "Rosa, would you please tell Nick that I've developed a rather severe headache. It's probably due to too much sun. I plan to take something for it and rest."

When Rosa left, Kelly went into her bathroom and found aspirin. Her message was certainly no lie. Her head pounded so much that her stomach was queasy. She carefully stretched out on the top of the covers and closed her eyes, feeling as though she'd been the victim of a sneak attack from a quarter she would never have expected.

Chapter Twelve

Nick looked in on Kelly several times during the day. Each time she appeared to be resting. He was worried about her. Rosa was also checking to make sure she had water and something light to eat.

After Rosa served Luke and Nick dinner that night, Luke asked Nick, "How is Kelly?"

Nick said, "She's been asleep whenever I've checked. Rosa said she managed some hot tea and a piece of bread about an hour ago. This is the first time she's been ill since we met. I wish there was something I could do for her." He met his brother's gaze. "I know I'm acting out of character, fussing over her. Go ahead and laugh if you'd like."

"I'm not going to laugh. I'm one of the few people still alive who knows your deepest, darkest secret."

"You don't say? And what's that?" Nick asked.

"You have a tender heart and you care too much about too many things over which you have no control."

Nick looked at Luke. "What drugs are *you* on these days?"

"Deny it all you want," Luke replied. "You're no longer buying up factories and other businesses just to make money. You want to improve working conditions for the employees."

"What a crock of bull. You don't know me as well as you think you do. I have a well-earned reputation as a ruthless predator who takes no prisoners."

"That might have been true when you were trying to reach the goal you set for yourself when you were fourteen. You intended to make lots of money... you've made lots of money. So why are you knocking yourself out after all this time continuing to buy out lousy owners? Why is this the first vacation I've known you to take?"

"Believe what you like. The reason I'm taking time off at the moment—and I'm still in touch with the office on a daily basis—is to spend some time with Kelly."

"You planning to marry her?"

Nick almost choked. "You're kidding, right? I'm not husband material. I certainly haven't changed *that* much."

"So this is just lust," Luke said with a smile. "More power to you, then."

Nick frowned. "Well, it's more than lust. I like her,

Luke. We're good together. We share the same sense of humor. She's intelligent as well as beautiful...and most of all, she's one of the few people I feel I can trust.''

Luke lifted his glass of wine in a toast. ''Here's to you, Nick. May your trust be well placed.''

Kelly stirred and opened her eyes when Nick slid into bed beside her. ''How are you feeling?'' he asked softly.

''As if I'm underwater, trying to move. My brain feels waterlogged and my body seems too heavy to move.'' She turned and faced him. ''Did you get Luke settled into one of the bedrooms?''

''Actually, I did have one of them prepared for him, but he told me he couldn't stay.'' He grinned. ''However, I did happen to run across a rather revealing portrait of me in all my naked glory. Still painting me behind my back, are you?''

She snuggled against him, her head resting on his shoulder. ''You weren't supposed to see that,'' she mumbled. ''Besides, it's quite obvious I wasn't behind your back when I painted it.''

Nick put his arms around her and buried his face in her hair. ''I'm flattered. I really am. Do you plan on displaying this one, too?''

She jerked her head back, bumping his chin.

''Ow,'' he said, rubbing his jaw.

''Of course I'm not going to show that painting. I didn't intend anyone but me ever to see it.''

He rubbed his hand up and down her spine. ''Will

you paint one of yourself in a similar pose for me? I'll hang it on the wall facing my bed.''

''You're incorrigible,'' she said, giggling. ''I will do no such thing.''

''Remember, I'm the guy who single-mindedly goes after what he wants until he gets it. I'll keep nagging until you do.''

''I prefer dealing with your nagging, believe me.''

She felt so good lying there in his arms and he wanted so badly to make love to her. He couldn't seem to get enough of her, no matter how often they made love.

Luke had been crazy to suggest that he might marry her, though. Instead, maybe he'd get her to move in with him. She could get used to his crazy schedule...and she would be waiting whenever he got home. He liked the idea of that. He liked it a lot.

''Kelly?'' he whispered.

''Um-hm?''

''I forgot to tell you. I came looking for you earlier today to tell you that I have to go back to New York tomorrow. It can't be helped.''

She'd been moving her hand gently across his chest until he spoke. She stopped and opened her eyes.

''Okay,'' she finally said, looking at him.

''Why don't you come back with me tomorrow instead of waiting until next week?''

She shook her head. ''There's no need. You'll be busy and I have a few things to finish before I go home.'' She traced his jaw with her finger. ''I've enjoyed your visit.''

"So have I."

"I'm glad we managed to clear the air between us," she said.

"Is that what we did? I would have said we scorched the air between us." He nibbled on her ear.

She sighed. "When do you need to leave?"

"Early afternoon. My flight doesn't leave Rome until evening. I'll have plenty of time to pack...and make love to you. That is, if you're feeling up to it."

She was quiet for so long that he thought she'd fallen asleep. Finally, she drew her hand across her brow and in a long-suffering tone, said, "Not tonight, dear. I have a headache."

Nick laughed and hugged her to him before he said, "All right. Not tonight. But all bets are off for tomorrow."

Kelly woke up a little after five. She slipped into the bathroom, then pulled on her robe and quietly left the room.

She'd known from the day Nick arrived that this day would come. She'd thought she was prepared for it, but it was going to be hard to pretend their time together had been merely a diversion for her.

Yet she had to do it. There was no way she was going to cling to him or expect their relationship to continue once they were in New York. She got a drink of water from the kitchen and stood looking out the window over the sink. It was too dark to see them, but she knew the rolling hills of lush green vineyards and other crops were there.

She was going to miss this place. She knew she'd never be able to separate the memories of her stay here from Nick's visit. Just for today, she would pretend that when he left, her heart wasn't leaving with him.

Nick returned to New York remembering the passionate send-off he'd received from Kelly. He already missed her and he'd only been gone a few hours.

Though it was late, he considered stopping at the office to see what Craig had left for him to look over before tomorrow's meeting. Instead, he went directly to the penthouse when his chauffeur dropped him off in front of the building. For the first time in his career he postponed getting back to work.

Once inside, the first thing he did was pick up the phone and call Kelly.

The next morning Nick walked into the lobby of his office whistling. The receptionist looked up, startled.

"Good morning, Mr. Chakaris," she said hesitantly. "Welcome back."

"Thank you, Mindy. Would you let Craig know I'm here, please."

"Yes, sir," she replied, grabbing the phone.

His secretary was at her desk when he walked into her office. "Good morning, Evelyn," he said, smiling. "I hope you had a chance to take some time off while I was gone."

"Good morning, sir. Welcome back." The woman acted like she'd never seen him smile before. "And yes, I took a few days to visit my mother in Vermont."

''Good for you,'' he replied. He walked into his office and closed the door behind him.

He glanced at his desk. Evelyn had kept it neat while he was gone and Craig had kept him current on everything that was happening. The place looked as if he'd been here yesterday. A good sign. He wasn't indispensable to the smooth running of his various holdings. He had good managers in place and Craig had shown skillful handling of everything that came up while Nick was gone.

Instead of sitting at his desk, Nick walked over to the window and looked out. He'd thought calling Kelly yesterday would ease the ache of missing her. Instead, hearing her voice and knowing she was so far away had made it worse. She'd been asleep when she answered, her voice soft and lazy.

He'd had an immediate reaction to the sound. Was his lust for her going to plague him from now on? He'd never considered himself particularly passionate about anything or anyone other than his career. Now his career paled in comparison to Kelly.

The door opened behind him. Nick turned and when he saw Craig he greeted him with a smile. ''Good morning,'' he said.

Craig closed the door behind him. ''For you, maybe, but you have the office staff in an uproar this morning.''

Nick frowned. ''What is it with these people? I just got here and I haven't done anything to offend a single staff member.''

''I didn't say offend. They're afraid that aliens kidnapped the real Dominic Chakaris while you were on vacation and left some whistling and smiling person in his place.''

"Very funny. I must say you're looking fit. The added responsibility must agree with you."

"Can't complain. Remember I've been serving at the feet of the master for several years," he replied with a grin. "I might have learned a few things," he added modestly.

They sat at the desk while they were talking. Nick laughed at Craig's remark. "Just remember that I may have taught you everything you know, but I haven't taught you everything I know."

"I live in anticipation, O Master, for the next installment of your wisdom."

Nick picked up the carafe of coffee Evelyn always had ready for him and poured each of them a cup, then handed one to Craig.

"You must be hot on the trail of a new acquisition," Craig said after a lengthy silence. "I've never seen you look this pleased with yourself before."

Startled, Nick stared at him a moment, then shrugged. "Is there anything wrong with being happy?"

"Not for most people. But I haven't seen you smile so much since I met you. It's kind of scary, now that I think of it. Maybe the staff's right. Aliens are the only explanation."

"All right. So I enjoyed my vacation." He paused. "Really enjoyed my vacation. I can't remember sleeping so much, eating so much and being quite so lazy before. It felt good.''

''Congratulations, Nick. You've finally learned what the word vacation means. Other trips you've called vacations usually managed to be with business associates, whether you were out catching sailfish in the Gulf of Mexico or skiing in Colorado.''

''Well, no more of that. I'm a changed man.''

''That's what I've been telling you since I walked in here. I'm stunned and amazed. So tell me, do the aliens intend to return the real Nick Chakaris to us or are you here to stay?''

Nick just shook his head, still smiling.

''Are you telling me that while you were in Italy you didn't show any interest in buying a farm, a vineyard, a factory?''

''Now that you mention it…''

Craig sighed dramatically. ''Whew, that's a relief. It's really you. Now let's see what you've found.''

When Kelly cleared customs the next week the first familiar face she saw was Nick's. She'd never been so glad to see anyone. When she reached his side, he nodded to his chauffeur, who picked up her luggage and led the way out of the airport.

Before Nick followed, he gave her a kiss that curled her toes and weakened her knees. When he finally relaxed his hold, she hung on to him briefly to regain her balance. ''Whew,'' she said, using her hand as a fan. ''What a greeting.''

He draped his arm around her shoulders and they walked toward the entrance to the airport.

"You look tired," he said. "What have you been doing with yourself?"

"Once you left I found that I had all this time on my hands. Since I wasn't sleeping much anyway, I spent most of my time painting."

"I know it's been only a week since I saw you last, but I swear you've lost weight. Good thing you didn't plan to stay longer. You might have wasted away to nothing."

She laughed. "Somehow I doubt that very much." When they reached the limousine waiting in front of the entrance, Kelly sighed and said, "As much as I love Italy, it's good to be home."

Once they were settled inside, he said, "Have I mentioned that I've missed you?"

"Mmm," she said, her head on his shoulder. "Let's see. I believe you mentioned it once or twice during every phone call. It's a wonder you had time to get any work done. I hate to think what your phone bill's going to look like."

He kissed her ear and trailed kisses along her cheek and jawline. "I'll see if I can scrape up enough cash to pay it before my service is cut off."

She turned more fully in his arms. "I really do thank you for picking me up despite the fact I told you not to."

"Yeah, I got that impression from the look on your face when you first spotted me waiting in the concourse."

"You really didn't have to, you know."

He studied her for a moment, then lifted her hand and kissed her knuckles. "Yeah. I really did."

By the time they reached her home, placed the luggage inside the door and sent the limousine away, Nick dispensed with further formalities by picking her up and climbing the stairs two at a time.

"My hero," she said.

"I couldn't do this if you weren't such a tiny thing. I don't want to wait to get you in bed any longer than absolutely necessary."

Once in her bedroom they set some kind of record for getting undressed and in bed together. The first time they made love was fast and furious; the second, slow and languorous and when they reached their climax together, they clung to each other until they fell asleep.

Rousing some time later, Kelly discovered they were still wrapped in each other's arms. "Nick?"

"Mmph?"

"I need to get up, okay?"

"Mmhm."

He didn't move.

"Nick?"

"Mmm?"

"I really need—" she struggled to pull away from him, "—to get up. Please let me go."

He roused to her last words and muttered, "Never" even though he opened his arms and allowed her to leave. While she was in the bathroom, he stretched and sat up. Clothes lay strewn everywhere and the bedroom looked as if a tornado had skipped through.

Nick gathered his clothes and got dressed. Kelly came back to the room, wearing a robe.

"Are you hungry?" she asked.

"Maybe."

"Let's go see what Bridget left in the refrigerator for me."

Nick was halfway through his sandwich and glass of milk when he remembered. "I almost forgot," he said after he'd swallowed a bite. "The Cystic Fibrosis benefit is tomorrow night. I've donated a few things for a silent auction and been asked to say a few words. I'm hoping you'll go with me."

Kelly's eyelids drooped. "Normally, I wouldn't hesitate but since I've just gotten home, there are several things I need to check on."

"I don't want to pressure you," Nick replied. "I'll check with you tomorrow afternoon and see how your day is going."

"Even if I don't go, why don't you come over after it's over?"

"I could do that."

"I've missed sleeping with you," she said with a hint of shyness.

"We can't have that," Nick replied, picking up his empty plate and glass and rinsing them in the sink. "I can stay tonight, but I'll need to leave early in the morning. I'll try not to wake you."

She added her dishes to the sink after rinsing them.

"Actually, I'm not certain it's a good idea to encourage you to sleep over, come to think about it. I might become addicted to you."

He hugged her to him and said, "I can think of lots of things worse."

Kelly waited until she'd had her breakfast and several cups of coffee, looked at her phone messages and visited with Bridget before going into her study to go through the mail.

There was a note that Greg Dumas had called last week so he must be back in town. She sat behind the desk and sorted through the pile of first class mail that Bridget had separated from the magazines and papers. As soon as she saw the return address on a large manila envelope she knew that this was what she'd been longing and dreading to find. She'd dreamed up several fantasies about her birth and why she'd been adopted. Now she would find out if any of them might be close to the truth.

The report was neatly typed and single-spaced. She began to read.

In minimal prose, Dumas gave her the facts as he found them.

The attorney, Calvin McCloskey, had retired but luckily was still alive. Greg hadn't been as lucky with finding Dr. MacDonald who had died a year or so ago.

He found out that both her parents were deceased. She felt a pang in her heart. Even though she'd never known them, she had visualized them as living, breathing people. Now she would never know why she'd been adopted, she thought before reading on.

Her mother's name was Moira and her father's name was Douglas. That was all the doctor had discovered before her mother had died soon after giving birth. Her father's brother had murdered Douglas a few days before she was born. No one knew her parents' last name or where they were from. Moira had been a stranger to the villagers where she'd given birth.

There were more details explaining the many steps he'd taken to discover this information. He'd certainly been diligent. He mentioned discussing the matter with the doctor's daughter and sister in hopes of discovering more, but none of that really mattered to Kelly.

Well...now she knew. If Dumas couldn't find anything more, she accepted there wasn't more to find. She picked up the phone and called his office. Once the call was put through, she said, "Hi, this is Kelly MacLeod. I just got home yesterday and read your report this morning. I'm impressed with your thoroughness, Mr. Dumas. I'm sorry that it took so much longer than we expected."

"Part of that was because I was under the weather for a while. It was colder and damper than I'd expected. So getting laid up for a few days prolonged the search."

"You're allowed to be sick, you know."

"Yeah, well, I was hoping I could buy you lunch and talk over some things I didn't put in the report."

"That would be fine. Where would you like to meet?"

He named a restaurant in mid-Manhattan. "I'll meet you there at one-thirty on Monday, if that's all right," he said.

"I'll be there. And…thanks again."

Kelly hung up and read the report again. Her parents had been Douglas and Moira. She wondered if the MacLeods had known them? If so, maybe it was her father's murder and her mother's dying so soon after childbirth that caused them to be so secretive. They were trying to protect her.

Or so she wanted to believe. Since she'd never know, she could believe whatever she wished about their motives.

With a sigh, Kelly laid the report aside, marked her calendar for the Monday meeting and slowly went through her mail.

As promised, Nick called in the afternoon. As soon as she heard his voice, she said, "I'm still on Italy time, Nick, and fading fast. I can't seem to keep my eyes open."

He laughed. "Poor baby. Then I suggest you get some sleep before I get there tonight because you may not get much afterwards."

"Promises, promises."

"And you know me well enough to know that I always keep my promises."

She responded with a theatrical sigh. "I'll see you later tonight," she said in a sultry voice.

"You keep that up and you'll see me as soon as I can get there. Play fair."

"I'll behave…at least until you get here."

"I'll get away from the benefit as soon as I can."

Kelly hung up the phone. She had never told Nick that she had been adopted. She had considered the idea once or twice while they were in Italy together and had decided against it. She still had trouble thinking about it, much less discussing it, without getting emotional.

She had shared so much about herself with him in Italy. Tonight she would tell him what she had found and about the investigator she'd hired. After she explained, she was sure he'd understand why she had waited until now to mention it to him.

That evening Nick checked his watch to be certain it was working. He'd looked at it innumerable times without the minute hand appearing to move.

Once the meal and various acknowledgements were over the small orchestra played for those wishing to dance. He figured this was the time for him to unobtrusively slip away. Unfortunately for his plans, various businessmen who wanted to discuss a project or get his opinion stopped him as he made his way toward the exit.

When the last person had walked away and he thought he could leave, he turned and found yet another man standing nearby waiting to speak to him. The man watched him and appeared amused about something. Nick knew he'd never seen him before. He sighed at the delay.

"Dominic Chakaris. I don't believe we've met," he said, offering his hand.

The blond man shook his hand. "Arnold Covington with Covington & Son. I'm the son."

Nick nodded. He glanced at his watch. He forced himself to concentrate on the man before him. He looked a little fleshy around his jawline and his eyes looked red. Where had he heard the name Covington before? "What does your business do?" he asked, resigned to being delayed once more.

"At the moment, we're spending most of our time and money fighting a hostile takeover. Or didn't you know?"

Nick frowned. "I don't follow you."

"My dad and I are fairly certain that you're behind the takeover, although you've covered your tracks so well, we haven't been able to trace the company back to you. At least not yet."

As the man talked, Nick realized that Covington was close to being drunk. He spoke slowly and carefully but Nick heard the slur in some of the man's words. Before Nick could comment, Covington continued.

"You haven't won yet, though," he said, making a mock toast with his glass before emptying half of it in one swallow. "We're going to fight you every step of the way. With Kelly in our corner, how can we lose?" Covington smiled brilliantly before finishing his drink.

"I beg your pardon?"

"Kelly. You know—Kelly MacLeod. Dad asked her to find out what she could about your plans and whatever other information she could glean from you. I figure now that she's back from her trip she's gotten everything we need to know." His smile turned nasty. "Pillow talk can be so revealing."

Nick felt sucker-punched. He'd dismissed the man's ramblings as those of a sloppy drunk until he heard Kelly's name. This slimeball knew Kelly? He must if he knew that Kelly had just returned from Europe.

Nick stared at Covington and saw his mouth continue to move but Nick heard nothing but a loud buzzing in his head.

He interrupted Covington to ask, "How do you know Kelly?"

Covington laughed. "Know her? We grew up together. Our families have known each other for years. Our parents were planning our marriage before we were out of diapers. So of course we knew Kelly would do whatever she could to help us out."

Nick wanted to plant his fist in the man's mouth and destroy the fortune's worth of orthodontia there. Covington grabbed a full drink from a passing waiter and watched him over the brim of the glass. He obviously wanted to get a reaction from Nick.

"As fascinating as this conversation is," Nick said, "I need to go." He started to turn away, then paused and added, "I hope you and Kelly will be very happy together."

Ben was waiting beside the car when Nick walked

outside. Nick felt chilled, in his body as well as in his soul.

Kelly was engaged. She'd been engaged the day she met him. Why hadn't she told him when he'd been so persistent about seeing her again?

Even a school kid could figure that one out. She had needed to find out more about his business. Playing hard to get had been carefully calculated to whet his desire for her.

And it had worked.

Like the biggest kind of fool, he'd gotten so wrapped up in her that he'd blindly chased her to Italy…where she'd greeted him with open arms.

All of it made perfect sense now that he had the full picture.

He couldn't say that she had lied to him about her feelings. They had never discussed their feelings. Hadn't she made it clear she considered their relationship temporary? She had never called him anything other than Nick. That should have been a clue to him. Once he'd been to bed with a woman in the past she would start calling him pet names—honey, sweetie pie and others too nauseating to think about.

Not Kelly. Despite her passionate response to him—and she sure as hell hadn't been faking that!—she'd never given him a hint of her real thoughts.

How had she managed to keep from laughing when he'd told her he trusted her?

He deserved whatever happened to him for falling for the person he'd thought she was.

Fallen for her?

Hell, yes! He hadn't known how far gone he was until he found out the truth about her. He felt like throwing up and his stomach was still roiling.

"Sir? Mr. Chakaris?"

Nick realized that Ben was speaking to him. "Yes?" he replied tersely.

"We've reached Ms. MacLeod's, sir."

Nick looked through the window and saw her home, the outside light illuminating the walkway. He'd been in such a state that he hadn't noticed where they were or that he'd told Ben earlier that he'd be staying at her home that night.

He knew seeing her tonight was not a smart move. He needed to adjust to this new information and see what damage he may inadvertently have caused the company. He hadn't intended to see her but he was here now. Maybe it would be better for him to have it out with her now.

Nick couldn't remember any specific questions she'd asked him. Nor could he recall them ever discussing a specific company other than the one her father owned.

Hadn't she given him fair warning that first day about how she felt about him. He'd been egotistical to believe he had successfully changed her mind. More fool, he.

Kelly had been careful not to wear an engagement ring, which made sense, of course. Explaining why she went to bed with him while being engaged to someone else might have been too much for her.

And…damn it…she had been a virgin! Something

else she couldn't fake. She'd been willing to prostitute herself to gain information from him. His stomach roiled at the thought.

Nick suddenly remembered why the Covington name sounded familiar. Craig had brought him the details of the company and what was happening there several weeks before he'd flown to Italy.

After carefully going over the portfolio he'd told Craig that he wasn't going after the corporation. A sound business mind was behind that business. The downturn in the economy of the nation had affected Covington & Son as it had most businesses. Where other businesses were closing their doors, the brains behind Covington & Sons had made the necessary adjustments to ride out the current market.

Nick had been impressed. Not one worker had been laid off. Instead, each member of management had taken a substantial cut in pay, something he'd never before seen done in the cut-throat business world.

More than likely, it was the senior Covington who was the brains behind the business. Somehow Nick couldn't see the drunk he'd met tonight doing much more than keeping the local watering hole in business.

The door opened and his driver said, "Would you like me to wait?"

Nick stepped out of the car. "Absolutely," he replied, looking at his watch. It was after eleven. "This won't take long."

Chapter Thirteen

Nick let himself into Kelly's home with the key she had given him. A lamp burned in the foyer. Light shone from under her bedroom door, which meant she was awake and waiting for him.

He quietly climbed the stairs and silently stepped into her room. She was asleep.

Kelly must have been reading…an open book lay on the bed beside her hand, the bedside lamp casting a soft glow on her sleeping face.

He came to an abrupt halt just inside the room as though he'd walked through an invisible magnetic field that had destroyed his rage and left nothing for him to feel but the excruciating pain of betrayal. Not sure he would be able to continue standing, he sat down in one of the nearby chairs. He was five feet or so from the bed with an unobstructed view of Kelly.

He felt as if a giant hand suddenly gripped his heart and was slowly and inexorably crushing it. He took in everything about her—her fine silver-blond hair, her delicate skin, the thick lashes resting on her cheeks and the slim fingers resting near her book.

What was there for him to say, after all? His pain was of his own doing. She hadn't caused him to trust her so implicitly. He'd done that on his own.

He'd known there was no future or commitment in their relationship so why was he feeling so much pain? The betrayal was part of it, of course. The sense of loss he was experiencing seemed out of place, somehow. He'd walked away from relationships before without looking back.

He remembered why he'd given up trying to convince himself that she meant nothing to him and had followed her to Italy…and how much he had missed her during the unending week until she returned to New York. All right. He knew this was going to be more difficult for him than he expected.

Kelly stirred and opened her eyes. When she saw him she smiled sleepily. "There you are," she said in a drowsy voice. "I thought I could stay awake until you got here. I'm sorry. I'll adjust in a day or two."

She sat up and held out her hand. "You should have come to bed when you got here. It wouldn't be the first time you woke me to make love with you."

Her words evoked memories of nights in Italy when he'd returned from Rome late and had crawled into bed beside her, kissing and caressing her into passion.

When he didn't respond, she frowned slightly. He

was far enough from the small lamp to be in shadows, which was just as well.

He cleared his throat, finding it hard to swallow because of the tightness there. "I can't stay."

Kelly got out of bed and came over to him, kneeling in front of him. She raised her hand to touch his face and he reflexively jerked his head away. "What's wrong?" she said softly. "Has something happened?"

"You could say that."

She had dropped her hand when he'd flinched but now she raised it as though to touch him anyway, then paused. She must have seen something in his expression because she sat back on her heels. "Tell me," she said calmly enough, but he could see her brace herself for unpleasant news.

"I met your fiancé tonight."

Whatever she'd expected to hear, that wasn't it. "My fiancé! What are you talking about?"

In a raspy voice he said, "I know that we've never discussed the change in our relationship that occurred in Italy. I thought you were involved with Comstock and that you agreed—" He stopped. There was no reason to rehash any of this.

"Nick, I don't know what you're talking about. I'm not engaged to Will or anyone else. I've never been engaged. What have you heard to make you think differently?"

"Arnold Covington."

She frowned. "What about him?"

"He introduced himself tonight and explained how the two of you have had an understanding for years.

He was good enough to tell me that the only reason you've spent any time with me was to help get information for his company.'' He saw her face flood with color and his heart sank. Only then did he realize he'd wanted her to convince him all of it was the ravings of a drunk and had no basis of fact. Her guilty expression verified everything he'd heard tonight.

He watched the changing expressions on her face and hardened himself. He'd dealt with corporate spies before. There was no longer reason to discuss the matter.

Still...he lingered. ''You can't deny it, can you?'' he finally asked.

''I've never been engaged to Arnold Covington. He sickens me. He always has.''

''Yet you were willing to spy for him.''

The statement hung between them like a chasm, separating them.

''Not once I got to know you and understood that—''

He stood and carefully stepped around her. Without looking back he walked out of her room. He heard her say something but he didn't need to hear more. He'd been a fool. At least he'd had sense enough not to discuss his present negotiations with her. No permanent damage had been done. That was the important thing.

His business was paramount in his life. All the rest could be dealt with. He opened her front door and silently closed it behind him.

*   *   *

Kelly shook too much to stand and she continued to kneel beside the chair where Nick had been.

She felt dazed. She'd awakened from a deep sleep and within minutes her world had crashed around her shoulders.

Why would Arnie tell such a lie? He knew exactly what she thought of him. Perhaps this was his way of getting his revenge.

How could such a worm be the offspring of a man as honorable as Hal Covington? Thinking back and reviewing her conversation with Hal, she wondered how Arnie had learned of it. Hadn't she made it clear to Hal when they met for lunch that she wouldn't spy for him?

Her guilt lay in the fact that at one time she'd actually considered spying for Hal. Of course after she met Nick she'd given up the idea. Would it have made a difference to Nick if she'd told him why she had agreed to accept his first invitation? And that she had changed her mind?

She'd hoped her wholehearted acceptance of him when he'd arrived in Italy would have convinced him how she felt about him. Of course she'd never told him that she was in love with him. That would have ended whatever short-term relationship they'd begun.

And now he wouldn't believe anything she told him. He actually believed that she would prostitute herself in order to discover his business practices! A surge of anger gave her strength to stand. With measured tread she went downstairs to turn off the lamp in the foyer. She checked the door first, made certain it was locked and set the dead bolt. She saw the key she'd given Nick yesterday laying on the ledge of the wainscoting near the door.

Kelly turned off the lamp and slowly climbed the stairs. She impatiently wiped her cheeks where tears silently slid down. She had nothing to cry about! She'd known their affair would be short-lived. Besides, there was no way she wanted any part of a person who thought so little of her that he'd accuse her of doing whatever it took—she believed those were his words—to ferret out his blasted secrets.

Who needed him? She certainly didn't. She reminded herself of that fact several times during a sleepless night as she continued to cry.

Kelly arrived early at the restaurant where she was to meet Greg Dumas. She was shown to a table near a window that looked out on a peaceful courtyard. She'd needed a little time to focus on the purpose of the meeting.

Not that she knew what that was, actually. Perhaps he wanted to tell her about the people he met. She didn't mind. She preferred talking about Scotland or anything other than Nick.

The redness was gone from her eyes and she'd taken care with her makeup. By the time she'd left the house she was grateful that she looked no different than when she'd met Greg the first time.

She smiled when she saw him walk into the restaurant. He spotted her immediately and strode to the table where she waited. He sat across from her and said, "I hope I haven't kept you waiting."

"No." She nodded to the menu in front of him. "Would you like to look at the menu and order? I know what I want."

"Good idea," he replied. While he perused the selections she studied him, trying to figure out what was different about him. Was there strain around his eyes? Did he look thinner? He'd mentioned having been ill.

After they ordered, Kelly asked, "Have you recovered from your illness?"

He looked surprised. "My illness?"

"You said you spent a few days at the home of the doctor's daughter." Now what had she said to cause his cheeks to become ruddy? She tilted her head, wondering.

"I'm fine. I received good care."

"Well. That's good to hear."

He dropped his gaze to his folded hands resting on the table. "The reason I suggested we meet is because I discovered something while in Scotland that I didn't put in the report."

"About Douglas and Moira?"

"No, unfortunately. However, while I was discussing the adoption with Calvin McCloskey he told me something you have a right to know."

"Which is?"

"The report stated that Moira appeared at Dr. MacDonald's home office already in labor."

"Yes."

He cleared his throat. "What I didn't put in writing

was that she was pregnant with triplets.'' He paused and took a drink of iced tea.

She frowned. Triplets. What did that have to do with—? Then it hit her. ''I'm a triplet?'' she repeated, her voice climbing in register. She stopped and looked around, hoping she hadn't drawn attention to herself.

''Yes. Moira had three baby girls that night.''

''Oh, my God.'' The news was almost as shocking as finding out she'd been adopted. ''But if there were three of us, why—?'' She couldn't take all of this in.

''Why weren't you adopted together?'' he asked, then sat back as their lunch was brought. She'd ordered a salad while he had one of the luncheon specials.

He took a few bites while she pushed greens around her plate. ''Sorry,'' he said, ''I skipped breakfast this morning.''

''Go ahead. I need some time to take all of this in.'' She nibbled on a small sprig of broccoli. His news would definitely take some getting used to. She had two sisters. She, Kelly MacLeod, an only child, wasn't an only child at all. She had sisters!

Greg put down his fork and sipped some tea. ''Because of what Moira told the doctor, MacDonald and McCloskey felt the only way to protect the three of you was to separate you. Moira had been adamant about hiding each of you. You were the heirs, she said, and her husband's brother would want to destroy you as he did your father.''

''What kind of heirs?''

''She never said. The attorney believes the reason

she didn't give her surname was that it would be recognizable. MacDonald told McCloskey she died without revealing anything more."

"Poor Moira," she said softly. "What a horrible time for her." She tried to picture a young woman losing her husband in such a horrible way, then giving birth to triplets. How could she condemn her for not fighting to live and care for her and her sisters when she had no idea what she would have done in the same circumstances.

"Oh, Greg, this is so exciting. Did you find my sisters?"

"I found one of them."

Kelly felt her heart leap. "You've met her? Oh, my gosh, this is wonderful. I have a sister." She leaned forward. "Did you tell her about me? Does she want to meet me? Oh, I hope so because I dearly want to meet her!"

"I met her, yes. Dr. MacDonald and his wife adopted her and named her Fiona. She's the woman who cared for me when I was ill. She has no idea she has sisters."

"I don't understand. Why didn't you tell her about me?"

"It wasn't my place to tell her. You're my client, which is why I'm passing on the information. It's up to you to decide what to do next."

"Fiona," Kelly said, tasting the name on her lips and soaking in the sound. "What a beautiful name." She gave up the pretense of eating. When he'd finished, she said, "Tell me about her. Do we look alike?

Is her personality anything like mine? I want to hear everything about her you can remember.''

She waited and when he didn't immediately respond, she added, ''She took care of you when you were ill. That sounds terribly romantic, you know.''

She watched him squirm at her remark. Oh, ho. What have we here? ''Perhaps it was more romantic than I guessed,'' she teased.

''I don't know about romantic. I understand she didn't find me a very docile patient.''

''Imagine that,'' Kelly replied with a chuckle.

''She lives in a cottage in the western highlands with her dog, McTavish, and a cat named Tiger. She's some kind of healer...I don't know how to explain it. She mixes herbs for teas and she has the most soothing hands.'' He came back to the present. ''You look very much alike. Where your hair is quite blond, hers is red. She has green eyes, not blue like yours. But your faces...yes, you look very much alike. You're both small.''

''Did you find out anything about the other sister?''

''Not much, no. A couple from Cornwall adopted her. I have their name in my notes, if you'd like to have it.''

''Oh, I think we should do more than that. I think we should go to Scotland together. It's obvious there is something going on between you and Fiona.''

''Oh, not at all. She was just a woman who—''

She stopped him with a grin. ''I'm very aware of who she is, thanks to your excellent and detailed description of her. It isn't what you said. It's how you said it. Even the way you say her name is revealing. So don't deny it, Greg. Whether you intended to keep it a secret or not, it appears to me that you're in love with her.''

He looked at her as if she'd slapped him...hard.

''If it makes you feel better, your secret's safe with me.''

''She smiles just like you,'' he said after a moment. ''It's strange now that I'm sitting across from you. I didn't notice the similarities earlier. If you had a Scottish lilt I would think I was listening to her.''

''So. Why don't we go to Scotland and you can introduce me to Fiona?''

''Uh, no. That wouldn't be possible. You can introduce yourself to her and explain—''

''Nonsense. I'm not going to spring such a thing on an unsuspecting woman who has no idea she was part of a multiple birth. You know her. She needs to be prepared to meet me.''

''The MacDonalds told her they had adopted her and that she was Mrs. MacDonald's niece. Discovering that her adopted parents lied to her will be very disturbing to her.''

''Really. Then that will give us something else in common, won't it?'' She reached into her purse for her appointment book. ''When can you leave?'' she asked, looking at her calendar. When he didn't answer, she looked up. He looked tormented. ''Don't you want to see her?'' she finally asked.

She saw him swallow. ''I don't think she's going to want to see me,'' he finally said.

"There's only one way to find out, isn't there? How about leaving this Friday. Will that fit your schedule? In addition to introducing me to Fiona, I'm hoping you'll go to Cornwall to find our missing sister."

He looked cornered. She almost laughed. She wouldn't be surprised if he was battling himself as much as her suggestion. When he finally spoke he sounded resigned. "All right. I'll take you to Scotland. But for the record, you're reading way too much into what I've said about Fiona MacDonald."

Kelly fought not to smile at his need to convince her. "Am I?" she said. "Well, we'll see, won't we?"

He paid for their lunch and once they were outside of the restaurant, she said, "I'll call your office with the information regarding our flight." She surprised herself by suddenly giving him a quick hug. "Thank you for bringing me such wonderful news. I'm in need of something positive in my life at the moment."

Greg gave a curt nod. "I'll meet you at the airport whenever you set up our reservations."

She watched him stride down the street, his shoulders telegraphing his discomfort by their stiffness. Well, well, well. Whether or not he wanted to treat this trip as though he were heading toward his own execution, she felt his being with her was the right thing for both of them.

Perhaps after some time in Scotland she would be better able to put Nick out of her mind.

Chapter Fourteen

"You look like hell."

Nick glanced up from the report he was reading and said, "Thanks," and continued to read.

Craig sat down across from Nick. "Oh, by the way, I heard on the news that California just broke away from the continent and drifted into the Pacific Ocean. It's now an island."

"Uh-huh," Nick agreed.

"And...there was a run on the stock market when it opened today. Your major investors sold their holdings and our stock is now worthless."

"Good."

Craig shook his head. For the past five days Nick had been in the office before anyone else and no one knew if he ever bothered to go home. For all Craig knew, Nick could be sleeping on the sofa across the room. If he was sleeping at all, which Craig doubted.

It was Friday night and Nick showed no signs of stopping for the day. Craig walked over to the bar and opened it. He filled two glasses with ice from the refrigerator and poured Scotch over the ice. He walked to the desk, set the glasses down and smoothly removed the report Nick was poring over, and then seated himself.

Nick had been studying the document so intently that he hadn't turned a page since Craig walked into the office. Craig suspected he would have been just as intent if the report had been upside down.

Nick blinked and looked at Craig. Before he could say anything, Craig said, "The whistle blew three hours ago. You're officially off work for the weekend." He held up one of the glasses and added, "Drinks are on you. Let's celebrate."

Nick's eyes looked terrible, Craig thought, watching him reach for the glass. Actually *he* looked terrible. Craig knew he had to do something.

"We need to talk," Craig said bluntly.

Nick swallowed his first taste of the smooth whiskey, licked his lips and took another sip. "Thanks for the drink."

"Did you hear what I said?"

"About California floating over to Hawaii or the fact that I'm in financial ruin and will be begging on street corners next week?"

Craig grinned. "At least you heard me."

Nick took another sip, a larger one, and slowly

swallowed. "I always hear you, Craig. Believe me, if I could put you on mute I would. What do you want to talk about now?"

"You."

"Now there's a tedious subject." Nick pushed back his chair, stood and walked over to the bar. He added more Scotch to his glass, picked up the bottle and glass and went over to the grouping of furniture near the windows. He sat in one of the large leather chairs and propped his feet on the matching footstool. "If I'm going to be harangued, at least I'm going to be comfortable. Why don't you join me?"

Craig moved to the other chair and sank into its comfortable depths. He set his glass on the small table between them.

"What's on your mind?" Nick asked after they'd sat and stared at the lights of Manhattan for a while.

"I told you. You. I'm worried about you."

"Don't be. I'm fine."

"Oh, yeah. I can see that. You're great. It radiates from you like a shining light." He shook his head and finished his drink. Nick made no comment. Craig poured himself another drink. "Here's the thing," he said after a healthy swallow. "Since I first met you, you've been one of the most self-contained, even-tempered people I know. No one has been able to tell what you're thinking…much less feeling.

"In the past couple of months I've witnessed you as tyrant, irrepressibly happy and now, as a walking cauldron of pain. It's obvious you're not sleeping…or eating…or doing yourself any good. Something's eating at you and you're having trouble dealing with it. For your sake, we need to talk about it…get it in the open…and whatever the hell it is, resolve it.''

Nick didn't look at Craig during his little speech. Instead, he kept his gaze on the window.

Craig leaned forward, his elbows on his knees, his glass in his hand. ''I'm worried about you, Nick. I've never been more serious in my life. You're scaring me.''

No one spoke after Craig finished voicing his concerns, and silence settled in the room. Craig turned on a nearby lamp and turned off the overhead lights, leaving them in shadows.

Nick finally looked at him, his eyes bleak. ''I'm having trouble with the fact that I've let my emotions dictate my behavior these past few months to the point that I've lost all perspective. Without being aware of it, I've placed Kelly in the center of my life to the exclusion of everything else—including my career—and ended up making a total ass of myself. I allowed myself to be royally conned by her, something I never believed would happen to me. I no longer trust my judgment or perceptions. I'm just dealing with a bruised ego, but I'll get over it.''

''Your ego, huh? You sure it isn't your heart?''

Nick reached for his drink. ''How would I know? I don't trust myself to know anything anymore.''

''What happened between you and Kelly?''

''I discovered Kelly's only reason for spending time with me was to get information about my current business activities to help a family friend. She says she wasn't engaged to him, but—at this point I don't know who or what to believe.''

''Engaged to whom?''

''Arnold Covington.''

Craig laughed. ''You're kidding, right? That loser is the biggest joke around. If you'd ever met him, you'd know that. Kelly would never give that bum the time of day.''

''Maybe not. But she's close to his father, who runs the company. If he asked her to help them out, which is what I think happened, she would do it.''

''So what did she learn?''

''About—?''

''I believe we're discussing the business...aren't we?''

''Nothing. Actually, we didn't talk about it.''

''So what do you believe she's done?''

''Made a fool of me.''

''How?''

''Well, she—'' He paused and carefully sipped his drink. ''Let's just say that she welcomed me with open arms when I showed up in Italy after giving me the cold shoulder before she left.''

''Is that all?''

''She didn't deny that she'd started seeing me to spy on me.''

''Maybe she thought you had enough brains to figure that one out for yourself. Obviously she overestimated your ability for sound deductive reasoning.''

''Meaning?''

''I don't know the woman. I'm the first to admit it.

However, she doesn't strike me as a devious or manipulative person. Correct me if I'm wrong here.''

"Well, I can't—"

"She made you the happiest I've ever seen you. It seems that everyone but you knows that you've fallen hard for her. So why are you so quick to decide that everything between you is a lie? Are you that afraid of being vulnerable that you'll grab at any excuse to dump her?"

"That's not what happened…and no, it isn't about being vulnerable."

"Okay. What is it, then?"

"She lied to me."

"When?"

"By pretending that she was interested in me…by painting my portrait so I'd be curious enough to meet her…by…" His words trailed off.

Craig waited, but Nick said nothing more. "Did you ever tell her you loved her and were interested in deepening the relationship?"

"No. We never discussed our relationship in those terms."

"Then why do you feel she should bare her soul to you about her feelings?"

"Yeah, well, I'm leery of commitments."

"Because you don't want to take the chance of losing someone else you love. I know."

"I've lost her anyway, so what difference does it make?"

"You know you've lost her because she told you?"

"I haven't talked to her. After the things I said to

her last weekend she'd probably hang up on me if I were to call."

"So not only are we dealing with a commitment phobia but being a coward as well."

Nick scowled at Craig. "Nobody calls me a coward, Craig, not even you."

"Okay. You're not a coward. Is it all right to call you a chicken?"

Nick reluctantly smiled. "I sound pitiful." He rubbed the nape of his neck. "That's nothing worse than being humiliated." He looked at Craig. "I'll admit I'm out of my depth here. I don't know what to do. Where do I go from here?"

"Okay," Craig finally said after another prolonged silence. "Here's what you do. Call her, apologize if need be, grovel if necessary and tell her you're so crazy about her you aren't sure that you'll be able to survive without her. Then go from there."

Nick shook his head in disgust. "Grovel, huh? What is it with you, anyway? That seems to be your solution for everything I do."

"Well, from what you've been telling me, it certainly sounds like you need to if you're convinced she won't talk to you. What, exactly, did you say to her?"

"That she, uh, used her favors to blind me to what she was doing."

"Ouch. You're right. You have the social grace of an orangutan." He paused, musing for a moment. "Actually," he said slowly, "I may be insulting the ape species. I understand they have well-developed and healthy relationships within their family group."

"Are you through insulting me? You sit here drinking my Scotch and giving me hell."

"I'll stop…if you'll call her." He handed Nick the phone.

"Now?"

"No time like the present. If you'd like, I'll leave and give you privacy."

Nick looked at the instrument as though staring at a cobra, wondering when it might strike. He glanced at Craig. "Don't leave."

Craig bit his lip to hide his smile. Nick sounded almost panicked. Craig sipped his drink and discovered the ice had melted. He retrieved more ice from the bar and added Scotch.

Nick picked up the phone and briskly dialed a number. Craig could hear it ringing. Someone answered and Nick said,

"This is Dominic Chakaris. May I speak to Kelly?"

He listened then said, "She left this evening? Why did she go to Scotland?"

Craig cringed at that piece of news. Nick would have a much harder time groveling with the Atlantic between them. He wished he could hear what was being said at the other end of the conversation. He watched Nick's expression, hoping to get a clue.

Finally, Nick said, "Thanks for the information." He hung up and looked at Craig with a dazed look on his face. "She's gone to Scotland." He picked up his glass and drained it. "I just found out that Kelly was adopted."

"What? You can't be serious. Nothing showed up

in her file to indicate that she was born to anyone other than Grace MacLeod.''

''Well, according to Bridget, she found out a few weeks ago. What do you bet she'd just found out the week she went to Italy? She'd been upset earlier in the week but she wouldn't talk to me about it.'' She could have told him later, in Italy. They had talked about so many things but never—not once—had she mentioned discovering that she was adopted.

''What does being adopted have to do with her going to Scotland?'' Craig asked.

''It seems that Kelly hired a private investigator to find out who her parents were and for whatever reason, he went to Scotland. He discovered that she has a sister living there, so she and the investigator have gone to see her sister.''

Nick could conjure up all kinds of scenarios with Kelly and her nameless, faceless P.I. Was he the reason she'd been so willing to treat their affair so lightly? Had she wanted more experience?

He scrubbed his face. He would drive himself mad with his jealous suspicions. Like it or not, he had no claim on Kelly, but he believed that she felt the same way as he did. He had known from the way she made love to him that she loved him.

Nick sat up. She *had* loved him, hadn't she? He wasn't making all of that up in his head. But what was he going to do now?

''You want to hear something amusing?'' he asked Craig.

''That would certainly be different.''

"She and her investigator left this evening. I missed speaking to her by a matter of hours…can you believe it?"

"Then you know what you have to do."

"I do? What?"

"Book yourself on the next flight. There's no point in postponing your groveling. Believe me, it won't get any easier."

Chapter Fifteen

Kelly restlessly paced the floor of her hotel room in Edinburgh. She and Greg had arrived in Glasgow at six-thirty yesterday morning, rented a car at the airport and driven to Edinburgh. As soon as they checked into the hotel, Greg left to get Fiona, looking none too happy about his mission.

There was obviously something going on between those two and she planned to find out what it was before this trip was over. If they had fallen in love she sincerely hoped that her sister's love life was in better shape than hers was.

She refused to think about Nick. He was her past…her sordid past, perhaps, the man who had made it clear that in his eyes she had no integrity.

He was history. Gone. Forgotten.

Well, okay, maybe not forgotten but she was working hard on that part. That's why she wasn't going to think about him. She needed to wipe him from her mind, starting now.

She stopped pacing long enough to look out the window. Greg had called her this morning to say he'd misplaced Fiona but reassured Kelly that he would find her. How could he have misplaced her? she wondered. He hadn't been gone that long.

Surely they would be here sometime today. If not, her brand-new sister would find her babbling incoherently when they were finally introduced.

Because she hadn't wanted to take a chance of missing them, Kelly had all her meals sent to the room. She was getting a bad case of cabin fever…but all of her waiting would soon be worthwhile.

This was the first time she'd been in Scotland and she looked forward to exploring the countryside.

Fiona. Her sister. The idea still felt new to her. She could only hope that Fiona wanted a sister. What if she refused to come to Edinburgh? Or refused to speak to Greg?

She didn't want to think about going back to New York and picking up the threads of her life there. Maybe she would sell the house. It was much too large for her. She and Bridget could find a condo large enough for Kelly to have a studio. The place held many happy memories for her but she didn't want to live in the past.

Kelly yawned. She glanced at her watch. Maybe she would lie down for a few minutes. She'd read the book she'd brought with her as well as the magazines she'd purchased in the hotel gift shop. She could rest until they arrived. Surely they would be here soon.

She stretched out on the bed, closed her eyes and promptly fell asleep.

The long-anticipated knock on the door woke her and she sat up, blinking, and looked at her watch. Amazingly enough, she'd managed to sleep for almost two hours.

Kelly jumped up and nervously patted her hair before she hurried to the door. An unexpected sense of shyness grabbed her and she paused, fighting a touch of panic.

This was it. Now she would know the truth. If Greg was alone then she would have to accept that Fiona had no desire to meet her.

She braced herself to accept whatever happened. She took a deep breath, affixed a pleasant—she hoped—smile on her face and opened the door.

Her smile disappeared.

"I don't *believe* this!" she said to the man standing in front of her door. "What did you do, plant some kind of tracking device on me? What are you doing *here?*"

"May I come in?" Nick asked quietly.

"I see no reason to invite you in. I believe we've said everything that needs to be said. Quite frankly, I have no desire to listen to anything you have to say. If you're looking for some kind of closure, go find it someplace else. I'm expecting company."

Nick glanced up and down the hallway and said,

"All right. Then I'll say what I came to say out here. The other guests might enjoy hearing it, even if you don't."

The arrogance of the man. Once again he'd proven to her that what she thought or said didn't matter. He would do what he'd come to do, one way or another. Talk about stubborn! He could give a mule lessons on the subject.

"Oh, all right…come in and say whatever it is that's so important that you had to come to Scotland to say it." She turned and walked back into the room.

Just what she needed. She'd wanted to be calm when Fiona arrived. Serene. Loving. All the things she hoped to find in a sister.

With Nick suddenly on her doorstop she would probably be growling, hissing and spitting by the time that fateful meeting took place.

His timing couldn't have been worse.

Kelly sat in the chair by the window, as far as possible from Nick, who had followed her inside and silently closed the door. He stood there, leaning against the door and watched her.

She had nothing to say to him. If he had something he wanted to say, then he could start at any time. She crossed her arms and stared out the window, refusing to look at him.

Her heart was pounding so hard she could almost feel it banging against her rib cage. She closed her eyes for a moment, visualizing green-covered hills, crystal clear water flowing through rocks, blue skies.

Unfortunately Nick stood right in the middle of her vision, demanding to be noticed.

Kelly could have sworn she'd sat there for several hours forcing herself to ignore him when Nick finally pushed away from the door and walked into the main part of the room. She couldn't keep from looking at him. He had on a black knee-length coat, which he had unbuttoned to reveal a black turtleneck sweater and black slacks. Who does he think he is...Zorro?

He took his time removing his coat. He laid it on the bed near where he stood and straightened. The sweater faithfully followed the contours of his chest, the very same chest that she had loved to run her fingers over. She had loved the reaction she got when she teased his flat nipples where they nestled in silky curls.

She knew exactly what he looked like beneath those clothes and could sketch him from memory.

Nick leaned his shoulder against the nearest wall, crossed his arms and ankles and looked at her without expression.

"Why didn't you tell me you were adopted?" he finally said.

"You came all the way from Scotland to ask me *that?*"

"That's why you were so upset the week you went to Italy." It was a statement, not a question. "Why did you turn me away when all I wanted to do was to comfort you?"

She unfolded her arms and clasped her hands in her

lap. "I didn't know you well enough," she finally replied.

"How about in Italy? I would think you got to know me very well while I was there."

"True. But obviously I didn't, since I would never have expected you to accuse me of lying and cheating and prostituting myself all in the name of big business."

He looked down at his feet. Hah! He had nothing to say to that, did he? He was a miserable worm and she hated him for not trusting her, for not believing in her, for not—

Maybe he felt the same way because she hadn't told him about the adoption.

"All right," she said reluctantly. "I should have told you about learning that I was adopted. I doubt that you'll believe me, but I fully intended to tell you the night you showed up breathing fire."

"Yes, well, that's the reason I'm here."

"What? To see if I'm having a flaming affair with Greg Dumas?"

"With who?"

"The private investigator who came with me to Scotland."

"Oh. Are you?"

"You wouldn't believe me if I told you."

"Try me."

"You're the only man I've ever made love to."

He almost smiled. "Good."

"Oh, I thought that would be good for your ego."

"No. It's good for my heart."

She frowned. What did he mean? With any other man she would assume that he was saying he cared for her, but Nick was never one to discuss his feelings.

He sighed. "The reason I came to Scotland is simple. I came to apologize."

The pounding of her heart stopped, skipping a beat, before it continued to race. Nick was apologizing? That was the very last thing she had expected from him.

"What, exactly," she carefully asked, "are you apologizing for?"

He straightened and rolled his shoulders as though to loosen tight muscles. "For accusing you of spying," he finally said.

"Ah. Then you still believe I was cheating on my nonexistent fiancé with you and then lying about it."

"Look, I know I'm not very good at doing this, okay? I'm sorry for everything I said that night. It was inexcusable. I know that. Of course you weren't cheating on anyone. I was upset and I said a lot of things I didn't mean."

Nick could no longer be still. He jammed his hands into his pockets and began to pace. Kelly had never seen him in such a state.

Finally, he paused directly in front of her and said, "Would it matter to you in the slightest that I'm so deeply in love with you I haven't been able to think straight since I first met you? I've been obsessed with you, surely you must know that.

"The mere suggestion that you intended to marry someone else made me a little crazy. My reaction had very little to do with my business. Once I calmed down and could think a little more clearly I realized that even if you *had* wanted to find out everything you could about my business dealings, it wouldn't have mattered to me. Because I love you. Because I've been so scared of loving you that I actually pushed you away.''

He turned away. ''I knew that night that I needed to wait until I wasn't so wrapped up in jealousy and fear to think about what Covington said. To analyze it. To consider the source before swallowing it. I've never been in love before. I didn't know it could eat you alive with doubts and fears. Believe me, I hate being so vulnerable where you're concerned. I've tried to forget you…several times. But each time I couldn't resist the need to see you again, to hear your voice, to touch you. I know I've been an ass. I just want you to know how sorry I am for what I said.''

Kelly didn't hear much of what he said after the words ''I love you.'' She had never expected Nick to say that to her. She'd never allowed herself to consider the possibility.

He loved her? Could he be serious? She stood and slowly walked to him, forcing him to stop his pacing. Now that she looked into his face she realized how tormented and exhausted he appeared. He was paler than normal, his eyes bloodshot and sunken.

''When was the last time you slept?'' she heard herself ask.

Nick turned on his heel and charged away from her. ''I wish to hell that people would stop inquiring into my sleeping habits! Damn it!'' He spun around and faced her. ''If this was about paying me back for buying your family's holdings you found a masterful way of doing it. I was stupid enough to believe that we had gotten past that. When you appeared so happy to see me in Italy I thought we were starting over and building a relationship. A committed relationship.''

In a quiet voice, Kelly replied, ''You've never been interested in having a committed relationship, Nick. How was I to know that's what you wanted?''

He stared at her in disbelief. ''Are you kidding me? Do you actually believe that this was some kind of casual affair we were having? Not being able to get enough of you and keeping you in bed most of the time should have been a clue that I was head over heels in love with you! Hell. I used to think I had a low sex drive until I met you. Now I feel like a teenager whenever I'm around you!''

He shoved his hand through his already rumpled hair. ''All right, so I never said anything to you and I should have. I would have if I'd had any idea that what I was feeling was love, okay? I've never felt like that with anyone. I didn't stop to analyze what I was feeling and find a label to slap on it. All I knew was that for the first time in a very long while I was happy…whether we were making love, sitting quietly reading…or just spending time together. How should I have known what all that meant?''

Kelly wanted to throw her arms around him and hug him. Looking at their relationship through his perspective, she could better understand what he had gone through…what he was still going through. She thought of the young boy he must have been, losing so many members of his family and feeling helpless to do anything about it. She had a hunch he'd packed his emotions away in an effort to bury his pain. He'd focused on work, allowing his intelligence and drive to keep him centered and moving forward.

Then she had come into his life.

She smiled. "You know, Nick, you should have asked your brother to explain what was happening to you. He had no trouble understanding the changes in you. As a matter of fact, he threatened me with dire consequences, hand-delivered by him, if I should ever hurt you."

Nick reacted to her words like a boxer who hadn't seen the knockout blow coming at him.

"Are you talking about Luke?" he asked incredulously.

"Do you have another brother? Of course I'm talking about Luke!"

"He talked to you about me?"

"Oh, yes. He did everything but ask me if my intentions toward you were honorable. I have to say, I wasn't prepared to have to defend myself to your brother. By the time he was through with me, I was fairly flattened and fully warned."

Nick looked dazed. "Unbelievable. Luke was grilling you? I haven't needed protecting for years. I can't believe he jumped into his big brother role now." He gave a sharp laugh. "Whatever possessed him to think

I would need protection from anyone? There are a number of people who would find the idea laughable.''

"He told me what happened to your parents and to your sisters. I think I understand now why making money was so important to you.''

"Well, Luke has certainly turned into a regular Chatty Cathy, hasn't he?

"Look, I didn't come here to discuss my business practices. I came here to apologize to you if I had hurt you in any way, to explain why I said the things I said, to tell you that I love you and to plead with you to marry me!''

His words reverberated in the sudden silence of the room.

They stared at each other. He wore his ferocious scowl while she stood staring at him with something close to shock.

"You want to marry me?'' she finally whispered.

"Yes, I do. Very much. As soon as possible. Although that wasn't exactly the way I intended to introduce the subject,'' he said, sounding defeated.

Oh, this man. It was going to take a great deal of understanding on her part in order to live with him, but that didn't matter. Nothing mattered except the fact that Dominic Chakaris loved her—he'd said so—and he wanted to marry her.

She sat suddenly on the closest available surface, which happened to be the bed. "How did you intend to mention the subject?'' she said, sounding a little breathless.

He sat beside her. He leaned over to his coat,

reached into the inside pocket and pulled out a small box. Without a word, he flipped open the lid and held the box out to her.

The old-fashioned setting grabbed her heart. A circle of diamonds surrounded a cluster of rubies on a golden band. She noticed that his hand shook slightly.

Kelly looked into the eyes of this man she loved as much as life itself and saw everything that he'd been unable to say—his vulnerability, his bewilderment at his vulnerability and the fear that she would send him away.

The surge of love she felt for him brought tears to her eyes.

"Oh, Nick," she whispered. "I'm having a little trouble believing this is happening."

"Do you want to marry me?"

She leaned into him, feeling his warmth and solid strength. "More than anything else in the whole wide world. I've loved you for so long but I didn't think you wanted to know about it. I've struggled not to blurt out my feelings to you whenever we were together. To find out you love me and want to marry me is so much more than I ever expected. I can't take it all in."

"I need to hear you say it, Kelly. I have to know where we're going with this relationship. Have you forgiven me for all the things I said to you? Will you marry me?"

She tentatively touched the ring that blazed so brightly in the darkening room. "I don't have a choice," she finally replied, her chuckle sounding watery. She brushed away a tear. "If I say no, Luke will track me down and hound me for the rest of my life."

Nick stared at her with a bewildered expression on his face. "I can't believe this. I come with my heart in my hand and all you can do is make a joke."

Kelly threw her arms around him, causing them both to overbalance and fall back on the bed. She leaned over him and placed her mouth on his, slipping her tongue between his lips. He held her against him, following her lead. Kelly felt a surge of love intermingled with lust sweep through her.

She was exactly where she wanted to be...in Nick's arms. When she finally pulled slightly away from him, she said, "I don't mean to tease you, but I'm so happy I'm giddy." She gave him a brief kiss. "I love you so much my heart overflows with it. In answer to your questions, yes I do forgive you if you'll forgive me for all the rotten things I've said to you since we first met. You were always the one who wanted to put the past behind us while I held on for far too long. It would give me a great deal of pleasure to marry you, Nick, the sooner the better."

He pulled her closer with a groan, making a muffled sound, and rolled until she was beneath him. She immediately slid her hand down toward his zipper and found him jutting against the fabric.

"I want you inside me, Nick," she whispered. "Now!" She slid the zipper down until he sprang into her hand. He slid his hand beneath her skirt and within seconds he was deeply imbedded.

They were both panting. "See," she said, "you've turned me into an insatiable woman."

He grinned. "That's good to hear. We're certainly well-matched." His mouth locked onto hers and he set a rhythm with his tongue that mimicked his thrusts. She couldn't get close enough to him. She wrapped herself around him and hung on, engulfed by so many sensations.

"I love you, love you, love you," she said over and over until he tightened his hold and she felt his release, which triggered hers. They clung to each other, trying to get air into their lungs.

Nick rolled onto his side, still inside her. "I don't want to let you go," he said hoarsely.

"You couldn't get rid of me if you tried," she replied, grinning. She wanted to laugh out loud with sheer joy. "I can get you for breach of promise and show the ring as evidence."

"Oops," he said raising his head and looking around. "I forgot about the ring."

"Mmm. That could be what's been poking me in the shoulder." He looked behind her and picked up the open box.

"Why didn't you say something?"

"Are you kidding? I didn't even notice it until we turned over just now."

Nick reluctantly pulled away from and then began to laugh.

"What's so funny?"

"We are. We didn't bother taking anything off. First time I've made love with my shoes still on."

"Me, too." She looked at him and they both laughed until tears were streaming down her face. When she could get her breath, Kelly said, "I'm so glad you came after me. How did you know where I was?"

"Bridget felt sorry for me. She told me when you left and where you planned to stay. I arrived within twenty-four hours of you but I knew I couldn't see you until I got some rest. I got a room and slept around the clock."

After adjusting their clothes Nick removed the ring from the box and slid it on her finger.

"It's so beautiful, Nick," she said.

"I wanted something that wouldn't look too big on your hand. I'm glad you like it."

"I suppose I shouldn't be surprised that it fits. I don't know how you manage to be so efficient."

"In this case, I really had to guess. It looks great on your finger."

She looked at him and tried not to laugh when she said, "I really want to kiss you but I've discovered a natural phenomena occurs whenever I do. I believe it's called spontaneous combustion. Consider yourself kissed." Kelly was so caught up in the moment that she barely heard the knock at the door.

The second knock was harder and she sat up abruptly. "Oh, my gosh. How could I have forgotten? They're here! At least I hope she's with him."

She slipped off the bed and made certain her blouse was tucked into her skirt. Nick stood as well and adjusted his belt. She rushed to the door, thankful they hadn't arrived ten minutes earlier.

This time when she opened the door she found Greg and Fiona standing there...a smiling Greg with his arm around Fiona's shoulders.

"Please come in," she said breathlessly, her eyes devouring details about this sister she'd never met. They were the same height. Fiona's hair was quite red and her eyes sparkled like emeralds. As soon as she saw Kelly she clapped her hands together and said, "Oh, Greg! You're right. We look so much alike!"

They stepped inside, both grinning, and Greg shut the door.

"I don't suppose I need to make introductions, but just in case—Kelly MacLeod, please meet Fiona Mac-Donald, who happens to be your sister. She's agreed to change her last name to Dumas."

"Oh, Greg, what wonderful news!" Kelly said. To Fiona she said, "I can't tell you how nervous I've been about meeting you for the first time." She took her hand in a firm clasp. "I have a feeling it's going to be all right."

Fiona's eyes filled with tears and she blinked rapidly. "Oh, yes. When Greg explained that the Kelly MacLeod who was his client was also my sister, I was stunned. I wish my parents had told me the truth about my adoption, though."

"I certainly can identify with that." She motioned them to come into the room. "We have quite a lot of catching up to do, but first, there's someone here I want you to meet."

Greg looked startled to see a man in her room. For good reason. He knew she'd never been in Scotland before. Kelly caught the speculative look in his eyes.

"I'd like to introduce Nick Chakaris, who flew over from New York to see me." She turned to Nick, "As you've already guessed this is Greg Dumas and my sister, Fiona."

Nick shook each of their hands. "I'm pleased to meet both of you." He casually placed his arm around Kelly's waist.

Greg narrowed his eyes. "Chakaris. I know that name."

Kelly laughed. "I'm sure you do, Greg. And yes, he is that Dominic Chakaris, entrepreneur extraordinaire."

Greg nodded.

"Kelly left out a little of the introductions," Nick said with a gleam in his eyes. "She's agreed to change her last name as well."

Chapter Sixteen

Three weeks later

"I'm pregnant."

Kelly and Fiona stared at each other.

"You really think so?" Fiona asked, her eyes widening.

"Oh, yes, I'm definitely sure now," Kelly replied. "Because I'm not very regular I didn't think much about it last month but now I know."

Kelly had joined Fiona in the kitchen where she was preparing food that smelled delicious. She sat down on one of the stools.

Fiona had suggested at their first meeting that Kelly come stay with her for a while to give them a chance to get to know each other. It had worked out very well. Greg had gone to Cornwall and Nick was in New York.

They had discovered during their long hours of conversation that their tastes in books, art, healing arts and hobbies were quite similar. They discussed their parents and their upbringing, sharing stories that made them laugh and cry...sometimes both at the same time.

Now they were waiting for the next phase of their lives to begin.

Kelly stared into her cup. "I can't claim to be surprised that I'm expecting a baby. I can probably pinpoint the day he or she was conceived. It was the only time we didn't use protection."

"How do you feel about it?"

"I'm fine with it, but I'm not sure how Nick's going to take it. He keeps making possessive sounds about the two of us spending as much time as possible together. With his schedule, that's going to be tough to arrange. And a baby coming along so soon?" She shrugged. "I guess he'll have to adjust."

Fiona set a cup of tea in front of Kelly and sat with her cup. "Greg and I haven't talked about a family, really. I don't know how Tina's going to feel about another child in the house."

"She's five, right? I bet she'll be delighted. From what you've told me, she certainly seems pleased that you're going to marry her daddy."

Fiona laughed. "Isn't she a dear? You would think she'd picked me out as her mommy herself."

"Isn't it strange how things have worked out? That we should find the men we love at the same time?"

"I never question fate," Fiona replied. "I think it's great, myself. I would never have thought that I would have a double wedding with my sister."

"We'll have a wedding only if the intended grooms show up in the next couple of days."

"I thought you said Nick would be here sometime today."

"That's what he told me."

"When Greg called from Cornwall last night, he said he was going to drive as far as he could before stopping for the night. He hoped to get in sometime this afternoon."

"Did he say if he'd found out anything?"

"Yes, but that was all he would say. He wants to tell all of us at the same time what he found out."

Kelly shook her head ruefully. "That's Greg. Always efficient."

They heard the front door open and Nick saying, "Anyone here?"

Kelly jumped up and ran to the front door. Nick had just closed the door and set his suitcase and briefcase down when she leaped on him, hugging him fiercely around the neck. "I've missed you so much. We've barely seen each other in the past three weeks!"

He laughed and swung her around. "That's because I've had to finish up some ventures that all came to fruition at the same time."

He kissed her hungrily before whispering, "Would

Fiona be shocked if I took you to bed in the middle of the afternoon?''

''I wouldn't want to find out, would you?''

His sigh was theatrical. ''Oh, well, I suppose I can wait a few hours.'' He pulled off his heavy coat. ''Some of Fiona's tea would help to get me warm, I suppose.'' He walked with Kelly down the hall to the kitchen, their arms wrapped around the other's waist.

Fiona was nowhere to be seen when they pushed open the swinging door. She'd taken her cup and disappeared. Kelly smiled, knowing that her sister was giving her time to tell Nick her news. She poured tea into his cup and refilled hers. ''The trip was all right?''

He tasted the tea and smiled with pleasure. ''Can't complain. How about you? What have you been up to since we spoke yesterday.''

''Well…as a matter of fact, there is something I want to tell you.''

Nick slowly lowered the cup and stared at her. ''If you're thinking about postponing the wedding, don't even go there. I wanted to marry you three weeks ago.''

''It's not that. Do you remember that day in Italy when we made love in the pool?''

His grin was wicked. ''Oh, yeah.''

''And we didn't use any protection?''

He lifted one eyebrow. ''Are you saying—?''

She nodded. ''I know you've been saying you wanted me all to yourself and I'll understand if you aren't too thrilled about the news, but I—''

''What are you talking about! Don't you know that

I was fully aware of what I was doing that day…and didn't care? I waited for you to tell me if you were pregnant. When you never mentioned it, I figured that you weren't.''

"Do you mind that we're starting a family so soon?''

He lifted her off her stool and pulled her into his lap. "Let me make this clear to you. I love you. I'm going to marry you. I want a family with you. Our firstborn is obviously in a hurry to join the family and I don't blame him in the least. We have a few months to—how many months, by the way?''

"My guess is he'll be here in about seven months. Or she will be.''

"Doesn't matter.'' He kissed her so gently that she turned into putty. "How do you feel about it?''

"It sounds selfish to say this, but I've wanted to have your baby for a long time. In fact, I was hoping that I might have gotten pregnant, once I knew you loved me.''

They were still sitting in the kitchen discussing the future when Greg came home.

That night after dinner the four of them gathered in Fiona's living room. Fiona and Kelly had been sharing frustrated looks because Greg had been silent about his trip since he arrived. Of course they understood that he needed to shower and eat something, but it didn't make the waiting any easier.

Two love seats faced each other in front of the fireplace. Nick and Kelly sat opposite Greg and Fiona.

Once they were settled, Fiona said, "Now tell us. We've been quite patient, waiting for you to eat and relax some. What did you find out?"

Greg looked over at Nick. He'd been surprised to discover that he liked his future brother-in-law. They came from completely different social strata, but when he'd discovered Nick was from the Bronx while Greg grew up in Queens, Greg realized that they had more in common than he'd first thought.

Nick met his gaze and gave him an almost imperceptible nod. Greg had spoken to Nick on the phone soon after he arrived in Cornwall. He'd kept him current on the investigation but neither felt Kelly and Fiona should hear about each snippet of information he'd managed to uncover.

He cleared his throat. "Well, I guess there's no easy way to say this but to say it. I couldn't find her."

Kelly and Fiona looked at each other in dismay.

"Here's what I did manage to get with McCloskey's help.

"The couple who adopted her were Tristan and Hedra Craddock. They lived in St. Just in Cornwall at the time of the adoption. I started with that address, even though I didn't really expect to find them there after twenty-five years.

"Thankfully the town is small enough that I was able to canvass the area to see if anyone knew where they were living today. I was told that Tristan's sister lived not far from town and that she might be able to help me.

"When I found the sister, she told me her brother

and his family had moved to Australia many years ago.''

Kelly groaned. Australia. They would never be able to find her in time for the wedding in two days.

''I asked if she had an address for them and she told me they'd died in some kind of flash food during a vacation in the Outback a couple of years after they moved.''

''She's dead?'' Fiona whispered.

Greg shook his head. ''Not necessarily. When the woman was contacted regarding her brother's death, she was asked to provide a home for his seven-year-old daughter. She said she told the authorities that she didn't have room for her.''

Stunned, Kelly and Fiona stared at each other in disbelief.

''You're saying she refused to take in an orphaned seven-year-old?'' Kelly asked.

''Yes. She did have eight of her own living at home at the time, she said.''

''But still,'' Fiona said softly, unable to continue.

Greg hugged her. ''I know, sweetheart. Her actions were unconscionable.''

Nick finally spoke. ''What do you suggest we do now, Greg? We certainly aren't going to stop searching for her, so what's the next step?''

''That depends. The four of us could go to Australia to look for her, but without knowing her name—''

''You mean the hateful woman didn't bother to learn her *name?*'' Fiona asked.

''She said she didn't remember. They'd been gone

a long time. The thing is, your sister could very well have been adopted by someone else since then and would no longer be using the Craddock name. Personally, I believe it would be a waste of our time to go searching in a country we know little about for someone whose name we don't know.''

''We've got to find her, Greg,'' Kelly said. ''We just have to.''

''I know. I think our best choice would be to hire an investigator in Australia who's familiar with the country. He'd have a better chance of finding out the date the accident happened from old records and perhaps get an address and a name. He could canvass the neighborhood much as I did in Cornwall and hope somebody knows something about what happened to her.''

''This is so strange,'' Fiona said. ''Both of our sets of parents drowned. At least I was grown when I lost mine.'' Tears trickled down her face. ''We must do whatever it takes to find her. It's even more important now than ever. She must learn that she has family after all.''

Nick said, ''Don't worry, Fiona. We're going to find her. The only question is when.''

Two days later Mr. and Mrs. Dominic Chakaris and Mr. and Mrs. Gregory Dumas greeted their wedding guests at the reception immediately following their wedding ceremony. Guests seeing Kelly and Fiona together for the first time continued to remark about how closely they resembled each other.

Kelly, who stood next to Fiona in the receiving line, squeezed Fiona's hand. After three very hectic weeks planning for their joint wedding, they had managed to pull it off, thank goodness.

Fiona turned and winked.

Tina's grandparents were next in line, offering their best wishes.

"I was pleased that Tina managed her part so well, weren't you?" her grandmother said.

"She was adorable. I'm glad she wanted to be our flower girl." Fiona had told her that Greg was getting his branch office in Edinburgh up and running and the older couple planned to go house hunting in Craigmor, Fiona's hometown, next week.

Only a handful of people came over from the States for the wedding. Luke was Nick's best man, and Anita, Kelly's college roommate, was her matron of honor. Hal Covington had come—without his son!— to give Kelly away. And Will Comstock had come.

Fiona's irrepressible eighty-year-old aunt Minnie gave her away. Minnie, Dr. MacDonald's sister, had been Fiona's only living relative until Kelly appeared in her life.

Kelly was relieved that Nick actually greeted Will with a smile and a handshake just now. Of course his other arm held Kelly close.

Kelly still didn't understand the cryptic conversation between Nick and Craig immediately after the wedding but since they were both laughing she wasn't particularly concerned. When she asked him about it,

Nick said they were merely discussing his future behavior at the office, which made no sense at all.

The line was dwindling and both couples were ready to be seated for their luncheon when Luke appeared in front of Kelly. He wore a dazzling grin that completely changed his looks. With a mischievous look at Nick, he put his arm around Kelly and said, "The best man gets to kiss the bride. It's a tradition."

However, the kiss he gave her was not at all traditional. He kissed her breathless, only releasing her when Nick punched him in the arm, causing the onlookers to laugh. Luke stepped back and said, "Welcome to our family, Kelly. Too bad I didn't see you first," which caused another round of laughter and applause.

The meal was everything she and Fiona had hoped when they chose the caterer. In fact, everything was perfect on this most perfect of all days—except for one thing. They both felt the absence of their sister.

Fiona leaned toward Kelly and whispered, "When does your flight leave?"

"Tomorrow morning," Kelly replied. "We're staying at a hotel across from the airport tonight for convenience."

"It sounds silly, I know, but I'm going to miss you," Fiona said. "Now that I know of your existence I'm finding it difficult to let you go."

Kelly laughed. "Don't worry. Nick has already promised to build a home near Craigmor where we'll spend much of our time. Thanks to modern technology, he'll be able to stay in touch with his office and take part in meetings without leaving home." She glanced at Nick, who was deep in conversation with Luke. "In the meantime, we have to make arrangements to put my house on the market."

"Is that going to be difficult for you?"

"If you had asked me that a year ago, I would have told you I couldn't do it. However, I've learned that hanging on to the past is pointless. I'd like to think that a new family with children to fill up the rooms and run through the house will give the old place a new lease on life. Otherwise, it would sit there empty."

"At least you won't be losing Bridget."

Kelly laughed. "On the contrary, she could hardly wait to get back to what she calls the green hills of her native land. She'll find visiting with her family in Dublin much easier from here."

Nick turned and said, "I hate to break this up, ladies, but I've been as patient as I can."

They both rolled their eyes and laughed.

He grinned. "Okay, that's not saying much. Let's just say that I want my bride to myself for the rest of the day."

Greg leaned past Fiona's shoulder and said, "I'll drink to that."

With as much grace as possible, the couples said their goodbyes. Fiona and Greg were going to Paris on their honeymoon, while she and Nick were returning to New York.

Several hours later, while she lay limply in bed with Nick sprawled over her, Kelly finally allowed herself to think about all the ramifications of being Dominic Chakaris's wife.

He'd pointed out that he didn't intend to spend much time in New York, but she wasn't looking forward to sharing him with his business these next few weeks. It was selfish of her, she knew, but she recalled how wonderful it had been to have the time together in Italy. With a baby on the way the amount of alone time they could have was measured in months.

Nick raised his head and gave her a quick kiss before shifting to lie beside her. "I haven't been quite up-front with you," he said. "It's confession time."

"I know. You have something new cooking that's going to keep you working overtime. Why am I not surprised?" She gave him a quick kiss and snuggled against him. "I'll adjust. You'll see."

"Actually that's not what I have to confess at all. I hope your French is proficient. That's the official language in Tahiti."

"Tahiti?"

"Our flight in the morning isn't taking us to New York. We're headed for Tahiti. I thought we both needed a chance to relax and enjoy a few days with little to do. I know the strain of looking for your sister has been difficult for you, not to mention your pregnancy. I think we deserve a Tahitian honeymoon with all the trimmings."

Kelly threw herself on him, straddling him while she gave him multiple kisses. "You're a mind reader," she said breathlessly. "You always seem to know what I need or want before I do. How wonderful. I've never been to Tahiti before.''

"And I've never been on a honeymoon before. Believe me, I intend to make the most of it.''

* * * * *

We hope you enjoyed
TOO TOUGH TO TAME,
Book II of Annette Broadrick's Special
Edition series, SECRET SISTERS.
Please look for the story of the third
sister, Jenna—who proves to be a match
for formidable intelligence operative
Sir Ian MacGowan—in Book III,
MACGOWAN MEETS HIS MATCH
(SE #1586, 1/04) next month.

For a sneak preview of
MACGOWAN MEETS HIS MATCH,
turn the page…

Chapter One

Jenna caught herself holding her breath. She consciously took a deep breath, exhaled and stepped into the room. Once inside she discovered a book-lined library that would cause an avid reader—which she was—to mentally salivate with anticipation. She almost chuckled at the idea of living in a castle with access to such a treasure trove of riches. The idea sounded too good to be true.

She took in everything in the few seconds before she looked at the man standing in front of the fireplace. Once she focused on Ian MacGowan, the room faded into the background. The commanding energy emanating from him inexorably drew her eye.

She immediately revised her mental picture of a white-haired elderly curmudgeon. Sir Ian bore no resemblance to such a person. For one thing, he was far from old—somewhere in his early to mid-thirties, she guessed. Instead of white hair, his was light brown. It curled riotously over his forehead and around his ears like a young child's—and looked so soft and silky her palms itched to touch it.

She had a sudden vision of a laird standing there, the family crest mounted above the mantel. Golden-brown eyes beneath thick brows scrutinized her. A noticeable cleft in his chin drew her eye and she thought he would be quite attractive if it weren't for the frown that seemed etched into his face.

"Come," he said, motioning his hand impatiently. "I won't bite you, for God's sake. Stop hovering at the door." He motioned to one of the chairs arranged in front of a brisk fire. "Sit."

Now that he had spoken, Jenna could better understand Ms. Spradlin's reaction to him. His deep voice sent a shiver of sensual awareness through her even while his manner of speaking irritated her. If she was going to be working for him, she needed to set some ground rules.

"Yes, I will, thank you," she replied graciously, crossing the room. "As you know, I'm Jenna Craddock and I've come to transcribe your work for you. However, I would appreciate your not using dog commands when speaking to me. I'm perfectly capable of responding to entire sentences." She held out her hand to him.

He looked at her hand in surprise before he briefly shook it. "Ian MacGowan," he muttered brusquely, his frown deepening. With exaggerated politeness, he said, "Please have a seat, if you would be so kind."

No eye rolling, she reminded herself. If she intended to work for the man she would need to adjust to his sarcasm and abrupt manner.

Once she was seated, Sir Ian limped to a nearby chair and carefully lowered himself, his jaw flexing when he bent his left knee. She made a point to focus on his face, most especially his eyes. When he made eye contact she smiled at him, folded her hands and waited for him to speak.

Abruptly, he said, "You're not what I expected."

Her smile widened. "You come as a bit of a shock, as well," she said, intending to voice her thought that he would be older. "Ms. Spradlin didn't mention—" That was as far as she got when he interrupted her.

"I'm sure my reputation precedes me," he said irritably. "That ninny Spradlin must lead a very boring life to get so much titillation out of my search for a decent secretary."

Oh, my. Sir Ian was definitely an irascible sort. "She mentioned that you've been without an assistant for a few weeks."

"Through no fault of my own, I assure you. The woman has an absolute knack for sending me the most inept or overly sensitive women who fall apart whenever I frown at them, raise my voice or point out a typing error. The last one left in tears, the silly thing. You're from Australia."

Jenna blinked at the sudden change of subject. "Yes, Sir Ian, I am."

He rolled his eyes. "Forget the title and call me Ian." He pulled at his earlobe. "I've asked Ms. Spradlin more than once not to use my title but she's too busy chattering on to hear me."

From her observation during the conversation in Ms. Spradlin's office, she knew he had been busy interrupting while Ms. Spradlin was speaking.

"I would think being a knight is a great honor," she said lightly.

"You would, would you? Tell me something about yourself," he said abruptly. "You're young, I can see that. Are you single?"

One brow lifted. "Yes."

"I don't want you to think you can move someone else in with you—married or single."

That comment didn't merit an answer.

"Why did you leave Australia?"

She held his gaze and smiled deliberately. "To see the world."

"Why Scotland?"

"Why not? I like it here."

He leaned back in his chair, staring at her from beneath his frowning brows. He had to be aware of how intimidating he looked. She wondered if he used that look to keep his employees in their proper place. She almost smiled at the thought. He might be laird of his castle but he would quickly discover that she wasn't easily intimidated.

What did it matter to him why she was there? she wondered. Perhaps he enjoyed irritating people.

After a rather lengthy silence while he stared at her,

he said, "Okay, now I get it. This is a joke, isn't it? Todd told you to show up here, didn't he?" He spoke in short, abrupt spurts. And his mind seemed to jump around like a grasshopper. She wondered if he was on pain medication. Being on drugs might explain his lack of focus and, to her at least, his strange remarks.

"Todd?" she repeated.

"Yes, Todd, my supervisor. He probably got tired of hearing me complain about not being able to find decent help and sent you to help out. Not that I'm bothered by the ruse, you understand. I need someone competent and Todd would make certain of that, at least. But there's no reason for you to hide the fact."

"Since I've no idea what you do for a living—other than write, that is—I have no idea who your supervisor might be. Why would you think I would lie about my reasons for being here? Are you always so suspicious of people?"

"Yes."

Great. Paranoid as well. He was going to be a joy to work with, she could see that already.

"Your story doesn't quite work," he said gruffly. "There's no reason that I can see for you to come to Scotland in the first place, much less apply for work. If you're serious about living in the U.K., London would be the most logical place for you to search for work."

Was this some kind of test? Was she supposed to break down in tears at this point? Calmly Jenna replied, "Do you have a particular reason for questioning my honesty, sir? You may not believe me but I have no reason to lie to you.'' She stood and ran her hands down her thighs to smooth her skirt. "You've made it quite clear that once again you're displeased with Ms. Spradlin's choice. I respect that. You certainly have the right to disagree with her.'' She picked up her handbag. "I do want to reassure you, however, that I didn't accept the position with some nefarious plan in mind. I merely wanted a job. Your family's heirlooms would have been safe with me.''

Jenna walked toward the door, mentally telling the rows of books goodbye.

"Oh, for God's sake, stop being so melodramatic,'' Ian snapped. "Come back here. I don't want to be hopping up and down every time I say something that displeases you.''

She turned and looked at him. "It isn't melodramatic to dislike rudeness, sir. I'm capable of dealing with a great many foibles, but I will not tolerate your disrespect.''

He pushed himself out of his chair and faced her. Their gazes locked and she, for one, did not intend to back down. She felt a small victory of sorts when he glanced away and muttered something that might have been an apology.

Or a curse word.

"Let's start over, shall we?'' he asked, running his hand through his hair. Definitely irritated, she thought to herself. Well, so was she. "Please sit.'' When she was seated once again, he said, "May I see your references?''

Without replying, Jenna reached into her purse and

brought out her resume and two letters of recommendation. After handing them to him, she waited for his next salvo.

After reading the documents, he looked at her and said, "According to this, your previous employer is convinced you walk on water. With this glowing recommendation, I'm surprised he allowed you to leave." He studied her for a moment. "Did your departure have anything to do with a lover's spat? Because if it did, I see no reason to have you settle in here only to receive an apologetic phone call from him that will send you scurrying back to Australia...with all due respect."

"Not that such information is any of your business, but since Basil Fitzgerald is sixty-five years old with several children and grandchildren, I doubt he could have found time for an affair...and if he had ever entertained the idea, Mrs. Fitzgerald would have bashed him on the head for considering it."

"If I seem to be prying into your personal life, Ms. Craddock, I do apologize. I need an assistant who will focus on my work. What you do on your own time is up to you. Just so we're clear about our arrangement, I'm not looking for a personal relationship with you. I don't have time for flirting or any of that nonsense. I need a skilled assistant. That's all."

Jenna fought to hang on to her temper. Fighting for control she studied the man, allowing her gaze to slide over him from the curls to his rather large feet. Eventually she raised her eyes to meet his and said, "Tell me, *Sir* Ian, are you always this obnoxious or did I luck out and catch you on a bad day? I can't for the life of me imagine why you think that I—or any other self-respecting woman, for that matter—would be interested in having a relationship with you.''

He looked startled for a moment, then gave her a boyish grin that was wholly unexpected...and devastatingly attractive. ''You'll do, Ms. Craddock. You'll do.''

Coming soon from

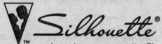

SPECIAL EDITION™

MONTANA MAVERICKS

THE KINGSLEYS
Nothing is as it seems beneath
the big skies of Montana.

DOUBLE DESTINY
including two full-length stories: FIRST LOVE by Crystal Green
and SECOND CHANCE by Judy Duarte
Silhouette Books
Available July 2003

Moon Over Montana by JACKIE MERRITT
Available July 2003 (SE #1550)

Marry Me...Again by CHERYL ST.JOHN
Available August 2003 (SE #1558)

Big Sky Baby by JUDY DUARTE
Available September 2003 (SE #1563)

The Rancher's Daughter by JODI O'DONNELL
Available October 2003 (SE #1568)

Her Montana Millionaire by CRYSTAL GREEN
Available November 2003 (SE #1574)

Sweet Talk by JACKIE MERRITT
Available December 2003 (SE #1580)

Available at your favorite retail outlet.
Only from Silhouette Books!

Silhouette®
Where love comes alive™

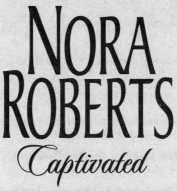

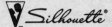

COMING NEXT MONTH

#1585 EXPECTING!—Susan Mallery
Merlyn County Midwives
Hearth and home were essential to Hannah Wisham Bingham, and she'd returned to Merlyn County, pregnant and alone, for the support of community and old friends. What she hadn't expected was the help of her *very* grown-up, career-minded best friend, Eric Mendoza. But Hannah had the perfect job for the sexy executive—as dad!

#1586 MacGOWAN MEETS HIS MATCH—Annette Broadrick
Secret Sisters
Searching for her long-lost family had led Jenna Craddock to the Scottish Highlands…and to Sir Ian MacGowan. The grumpy British intelligence agent hired Jenna to be his secretary—never expecting the high-spirited beauty to be the woman he never knew he needed. But could Ian convince Jenna his intentions were true?

#1587 THE BLACK SHEEP HEIR—Crystal Green
Kane's Crossing
As the newfound illegitimate son of the powerful Spencer clan, Connor Langley was forced to choose between proving his loyalty to his new family by getting Lacey Vedae to give up her coveted Spencer land, or devoting himself to the sweet and vulnerable Lacey, who was slowly invading his jaded heart.

#1588 THEIR BABY BOND—Karen Rose Smith
She wanted a child, not a husband. So Tori Phillips opted for adoption. And she unexpectedly found support for her decision from her teenage crush, Jake Galeno. Jake became her confidant through the whole emotional process…acting almost as if he wanted a family, too.

#1589 BEAUTICIAN GETS MILLION-DOLLAR TIP!—Arlene James
The Richest Gals in Texas
Struggling hairstylist Valerie Blunt had a lot on her mind—well, mainly, the infuriatingly attractive Fire Marshal Ian Keene. Ian set fires in Valerie whenever he was near, but the little matter of the cool million she inherited made their relationship a million times more difficult!

#1590 A PERFECT PAIR—Jen Safrey
Josey St. John was made for motherhood, and in search of the perfect husband. Her best friend, Nate Bennington, believed he could never be a family man. But Josey soon realized it was Nate she wanted. Could she prove to Nate his painful past wouldn't taint their future as a family?